Attribution

Social and Cyber Spaces

By: Taiye Lambo

As Told To: Amanda Holloman

Contents

Chapter 1: Birthday Celebration

January 4, 2020

Rays of the sweet Atlanta, Georgia sun floated through the window over Benjamin Smith's full-sized bed and warmed his ebony face. Deeply inhaling, Ben allowed the air to fill his young lungs, holding it for a few seconds. As he exhaled through his mouth, his eyelids lightly fluttered. He focused on the picture of his family above his closet door. A light smile illuminated his face as he looked around his bedroom in anticipation. It was tradition that his parents got him a few smaller gifts and hid them in his room before his birthday celebration. Cool designer socks, a favorite candy or money were all possible hidden treasures. Anxiously, he jumped up in search of goodies. He spotted an anomaly across his room and went closer. As Benjamin sat in satisfaction, he closely inspected the gift bag his parents had hidden under the clothes next to his mirror. The orange bag contained Nike socks, underwear, white t-shirts and a fourth generation iPod. *Cool, an iPod with color display. How'd they get this?* He was very up to date on the latest technology and knew this would not be released for another 5 months.

In the distance, he could hear his parents downstairs with a familiar voice. The splendid smell of his mom's homemade French toast and crispy bacon. Just as the aroma was becoming too enticing, his stomach growled, prompting him to go join his family. A chill ran over his skin as his feet slapped against the glossy wood stairs. "Mom! Dad! Guess who's up?" Ben announced turning the corner into the kitchen. However, he abruptly paused in his tracks when he saw his uncle James sitting at the breakfast table. "Uncle James!" He exclaimed, running towards to him.

"Benny, my boy!" Uncle James stood to greet Ben. They warmly embraced each other, for it had been months since Ben's favorite uncle had been in town. James Conway was in town doing some work for a local Defense Contractor.

"What brings you in, Unc?"

"Business as usual. But your mother told me it was your birthday, so I stayed a little later for you, champ. You ready for today? How old are you turning? Eight, right?" Uncle James laughed.

"Unc, you know I'm turning 14!" he replied, sitting at the table.

"Ahh, yeah that is right. You're almost a grown man now, Benny."

"He's still my little baby and will remain my baby forever," Ben's mother interjected. She placed the plate of French toast, eggs with cheese, bacon, grits and strawberries in front of Ben. It was his favorite breakfast meal and his mom made sure to always make for him on special mornings. Everyone was seated and grabbed each other's hand with bowed heads as Ben's father began to bless the food. Once the prayer was finished, the family dug into their food, enjoying the savory flavors and light conversation.

"So, Benny Boy, what's your birthday wish? I know you have one."

"Just the party mom and dad are throwing me. I just want to be with my friends and y'all."

Uncle James nodded in approval. "Okay, so what gift is at the top of your wish list?"

"A laptop! A gaming one with a good graphics card and lots of memory. I need the best." Ben glanced over at his parents. "No offense, mom and dad. I love the desktop you got me, but I need something mobile now. I have business to handle like Uncle James."

Light chuckles were emitted in response to Ben's admiration for his uncle. "Well, dreams do come true so be careful what you wish for, my boy."

It was two o'clock when Ben's friends, neighbors and church family started arriving to the house. Colorful streamers, balloons and confetti decorated the walls. All the children were in the media room playing virtual reality games and the adults were in the living room talking. Uncle James was standing at the doorway, watching the kids defend their virtual castles from intruders before him and Ben caught eyes. Uncle James called him over and asked him to go and get the extra headset upstairs in his room. Quickly, Ben raced to his room, trying not to miss any of the action. As soon as Ben entered his room, a new unboxed laptop was on his bed. *Now this is my kind of surprise!* Running back to the living room, Ben wanted to make sure the laptop was his before he got too excited.

"It's yours, Benny. I already ran it past your parents so don't worry. But this is your first laptop and it's like a loaded gun. You can use it for good or bad. I hope you choose to use it for good and make a positive difference in the world." Uncle James was not much of a technologist, but he appreciated the desire of his nephew to have his own personal laptop. Ben's parents agreed to put the necessary safeguards in place on their home network to ensure that Ben would use the laptop in a safe and secure manner.

"Thanks, Unc. I really appreciate this. You won't regret it!" And with that, Ben ran back upstairs to be alone with his new prized possession. This birthday was the best. Once he was safely away from all the celebratory commotion, Ben immediately started setting up and customizing his laptop. He was so engulfed in the task at hand that he didn't hear his mom come up behind him.

"Benjamin, what are you doing inside your room while your friends are here for your birthday?" His mom asked with her neatly manicured hands resting on her hips.

"I'm just excited about finally getting my laptop," Ben replied with pleading eyes. He always had a knack for technology.

"Well baby boy, there is a place and time for everything. Right now, you need to be downstairs having fun with your friends who are waiting for you to cut your birthday cake and take photos with you. You will have plenty of time tomorrow afternoon after church to get more acquainted with your little friend, okay?"

Reluctantly, Ben pulled himself away from his portal to the world and followed his mother back to the party. When his friends spotted him, they all questioned where he disappeared to, giving him the chance to rave about his new laptop. All of their little faces were green with envy as he continued describing the machine.

"That's the most powerful laptop you can buy right now. It is the same one that my dad uses for his high-tech work. You sure are so lucky to have that, Ben!" One of his friends exclaimed.

This only excited Ben more about his gift. He was beaming with smiles from all directions. "I have a loaded laptop. It's very powerful and I'm going to change the world with this laptop!" He shouted out to his friends, remembering what Uncle James had said.

The rest of Ben's birthday party went by smoothly. He received so much love from all his friends and parents. An assortment of delectables graced the long dinner table. There were mini sub sandwiches, fruit and a variety of his favorite chips. On the side was a mountain of brightly colored boxes and gift bags. His mom and dad got him a new bike, Xbox 360 and NBA Live to accompany it, some Nike tracksuits, shoes, clothes and a 14-ct. gold chain with a cursive *BJ*. That night, he went to sleep with plans for his laptop dancing in his head.

Usually, Ben would sleep in until his mother came to wrestle him up to prepare for church; however, this morning, he was up way earlier than his parents to tinker with his new laptop. Scrounging around the web, he was able to download his favorite games and apps for free. Time seemed to fly by because before he knew it, his mother was leaning against his door frame. She was surprised to find him active so early.

"Early morning business to handle, huh?" She joked, coming to stand behind him at his desk. She examined all the test papers and homework marked with large, red A's on them. She couldn't be prouder of her intelligent son.

"Yeah, mom. Just handling some business," He joked back, looking up at her.

"Well, you have 30 minutes to get ready for church and meet us downstairs at the breakfast table. You better not be late, little boy or I'll have to handle my own business." She smiled at him, kissed the black curls on top of his head and left his room. He dressed up quickly and was at the table with his laptop. His parents joined him soon after and were on the way to worship.

While at church, Ben couldn't help but whisper to his friends about his laptop during service. Once it was over, some of the older members asked him if he enjoyed his special day and of course, he told them all about his favorite gift. Ben had a great time at church. After the family lunch, Ben rushed to finish his homework. This was a great weekend.

Ben was up before the sun Monday morning so he could get in some extra free time before school. As the sun began to make its journey into the sky, his mother entered the room. "Benjamin, you know it's time for school. Don't make this a habit. Now get ready. We only have a few minutes." She rushed, stopping by his room before finishing her own morning routine.

"Sorry, Mom!" He yelled after her. He mumbled to himself *Let me hurry up before she gets any ideas.* It would destroy him if she took his laptop as a punishment for not listening. He threw on his uniform, tossed his laptop in his backpack and headed downstairs for his mom to drop him off at school.

The bell that signified homeroom sounded loudly as Ben rushed to his seat in the second row. There about 30 minutes of free time before classes started and Ben already knew what he needed to do. Surveying his peers, he asked Sasha, who sat behind him, if she had an access code to the Wi-Fi. Unfortunately, Sasha and the few others he questioned weren't even aware of what he was talking about. The school's policy stated that all students, faculty and staff needed individual pre-authorization to connect personal devices to the secure Wi-Fi. This could be obtained through an enrollment process that required the IT department to scan the devices to ensure that there was not any malicious files, software or malware installed. Ben was hesitant in trusting his laptop with strangers for a whole 24 hours, knowing his recent downloads did not authenticate origin. *Great, a challenge.*

The dismissal bell struck, signaling to students that it was now first period and to head to the designated locations. Ben had math next, but he desperately needed an access code to tinker around on his laptop. Deciding to make a quick detour, Ben slowly strolled past the entrance to the IT Support department, eyeing the notice board behind the locked glass door. There were several brightly colored squares arranged on the board next to flyers and other memorandums. *Maybe one of those have a code I can use.* He had 5 minutes left before he would be considered late. Luckily, Mrs. Matthews took a liking to him and wouldn't mind if he told her he stopped by the restroom.

Ben twisted the knob only to find that the door was locked. Knocking lightly on the glass, he peaked around to see if any of the staff were present. An older gentleman greeted him but stopped him at the door.

"Can I help you, young man?" The man's bushy nose hairs, handlebar mustache and thick glasses looked like a costume to him.

"Uh, yes sir. I was trying to see if I could collect my Wi-Fi password real quick," Ben replied, thinking on his feet.

"Do you have a copy of the authorization approval form?" Ben gave him a confused look. "It was a yellow paper?" The man explained before shaking his head.

"No sir, I didn't receive that. I spoke with the other kid who's normally here and they said just come pick it up."

"Well, just wait here one moment. I'll go check in the back then." The man grumbled something under his breath about student workers and disappeared into the back, leaving Ben alone.

Ben looked up and around for surveillance cameras and was pleased not to find any. He pulled out his phone from his jacket's pocket and snapped a picture of the board. As Ben slid the phone back to its hiding place, the IT guy returned. "Hey kid, I didn't see any open request. Are you sure you--''

"Sorry sir, but I really have to leave for my next class now. I don't want to be late again. I'll stop by later on if I still need your help. Thank you for looking, though." Ben rushed out of the office and towards his class. His adrenaline was pumping and the feeling of excitement flowed freely throughout his body. *I don't know what this is, but I like it.* Stopping at the door of Mrs. Matthews, he zoomed in to get a better look of the picture. The top left sticky note was labeled "Guest Access Code". *Bingo.*

"Good morning class. Before we start our lesson, I'll have to go to the office to collect the materials. I need you all to behave while I'm gone. Sasha, let me know if anyone decides to act up. They'll be taking a trip to the office too." And with that, she exited the room.

As soon as the door closed, Ben brought the laptop out of his book bag. The code successfully logged him on the web. Ben felt on top of the world that he had managed to bypass the school's authorization process. *I didn't do anything wrong. They should just be more discrete.*

Ben didn't even blink as his browser automatically connected to his desired site. A small smirk graced his lips as he thought about his social engineering skills of obtaining the guest access code. *Now let's check these grades.* He logged into the schools site where all his teachers submitted their grades. Science? A. Math? A. English? A. History? A. Computer labs? A. Everything being to his liking left him feeling extremely satisfied. He liked being smart but was humble enough to not let it go to his head. Everyone is smart in a special way, his just happened to be academics and technology. There was always something more he could learn or do to appease his hunger for knowledge. Now he was realizing that a structured learning setting was only but so much help. This pushed him to discover new avenues; to seek new mentors, peers and teachers elsewhere.

On the following Monday, a three-page science report would be due for Ben's class. Hating to procrastinate, Ben was diligently working on his paper before a "Low Storage" message appeared in the top corner of his laptop screen. *Well this is going to be a problem.* Clicking to further examine it, he discovered over 50% of the space on his hard drive was being used for software. He released a low groan. Low memory meant slower runtime and possibly a crash. Twisting his lips into a tight ball, he pulled them to the left in contemplation. Asking his parents for an external hard drive would be out of the equation since his birthday had just passed. *The cloud.* Scrolling

through a few free storage sites, he found some that did not
require you to set up an account. *Seems secure to me. I just
need space for my games anyway.* However, unbeknownst
to Ben, this magically convenient storage was somewhere
on his school's server. It had been recently hacked and
portrayed online as "trusted storage for those in need". This
systematic leak had not yet been identified but it was only a
matter of time until it was. As for now, Ben was content
with having anonymous storage and access to his files.

Over the next couple of weeks, Ben continues stashing
his games, miscellaneous files and software in the virtual
locker. During this time, Ben had become quite acquainted
with various areas of the web that he had never been
exposed to before. He knew the passcode to the blocks his
parents placed on the network and had VPNs on handy if
they decided to check his activity. *Glad I remember their
anniversary.* Whispers of secret channels online like TOR
Networks and IRC chat rooms encouraged him to spend
much of his time there networking and gathering
underground finesse. How to download free software and
obtain authorization codes to bypass licensing fees were
just added to his young resume.

TOR offered a VPN for faster internet travels instead of
its traditional slower service that interested Ben. With this
VPN, he was able to reach private sites that permitted
communication with some peculiar, technology enthusiasts
from all around the world. The dark web was an obscured
place where hackers, salesmen and customers all searched
for their desired secrets. However, he was aware that
navigating these waters meant that he would encounter both
good and bad hackers. There were villains in real life so of

course there would be some crawling the web. Comprehending this concept influenced his levels of trust towards the kind of virtual pals he chatted with. People that used their advanced knowledge to help others and spread awareness were the kind he wanted to associate with.

Ben entered a local area chat based on GPS location and found that some of the students from his school and neighborhood were present. It had become a regular routine for him to sit for hours chatting and exploring with his online buddies. There, he felt understood and not treated like a child. He was becoming a young man and wanted to be treated as such.

> **supermarioman:** @BigBeeKnee u should join our pizza party 2moro at 5
> **BigBeeKnee:** where?
> **supermarioman:** my dad owns a gaming store on Lakeside. We meet there every Wednesday
> **BigBeeKnee:** cool. I'll see if i can stop by.

Just as Ben got ready to start a conversation thread on some of the newly released games, his mother called him down for dinner. Shutting the laptop, he smiled to himself. He was finally stepping into his own.

Chapter 2: Darkness Appears

Wednesday morning could not have come soon enough for Benjamin as he sat up straight in bed before his alarm had the chance to go wake him. The past two days seemed to drag on while he anticipated his afterschool plans. His complete outfit was hung neatly in his closet. He had to be fresh and presentable to meet his online buddies. The straight leg, dark Levi's denim complimented the red Ralph Lauren Polo sweater his mother bought him. She had also bought him matching Nike's that were still in the box. Excited for his day, he jumped up to perform his morning routine. After last week, his mom decided he was old enough to no longer need her to instruct him.

"Mom? Dad?" Ben called out as he walked down the stairs and into the kitchen. Usually his parents would have gospel music or old school jams playing from the Bluetooth speakers. This morning was quiet and still. Something in the air did not seem right. Coming around the corner, he found his mom sitting at the table with her head resting in her hands. Her long black hair covering her face. He looked around noticing no breakfast, lunch nor snacks were prepared for him. "Um, mom?" he called out in a low voice afraid to disturb her. She did not budge. Walking closer, he laid his hand on her shoulder. "Mom, are you okay?"

Kimberly Smith released a deep sigh, shutting her eyes as tight as possible before tears slipped out. Faking a yawn, she pulled her head up from her palms to look at her son. Her baby Benny. He was her pride and joy. A beautiful fruit from the love she and her husband bore. A small smile rested on her lips as she put on her best face. "Good morning, son. I didn't hear you come in." She stood up, looking around the counter for her keys. "How did you sleep? Ready for school?"

Ben inspected his mother. He knew something was off about her. "Yeah, I slept fine. I'm wearing the sweater you got me," he said in attempts to lift her spirits. She loved fashion and him looking nice always filled her with joy.

"That's nice, baby. I'm glad it fits you. You ready to go?" she rushed him walking towards the door.

"Ma, you didn't make me breakfast or anything," he commented, looking at her strangely.

Kim's fingers pinched the bridge of her nose and shut her eyes again. *Get it together, girl. You're slipping.* "I'm sorry, baby. It was a long night writing reports for the company. Big presentation coming up," she lied. "We can pick you up something along the way. How about a chicken biscuit?"

"Yeah, that's fine. What about lunch? You know the school's lunch is scary," he joked, attempting to lighten the mood.

She gave him a lighthearted chuckle. "Will a ten be enough to buy you something from the cafe?" Ben nodded eagerly. She had never given him more than five so the leftover could be used later after school. With that, they headed out.

Once Ben arrived at school, he pushed the thoughts of his mom to the back of his mind. There had been days before where she had been off and he figured that tomorrow would be better. His concern now was surviving the mundane school drills. Classes were boring. The food was suspicious. And well, everybody else just went along with it all. Ben craved excitement. Life as he knew it was just regular shmegular. Nothing made the school seem challenging to him. As he walked through the halls towards his homeroom, he nodded at a few of his friends. Lost in thought, Ben did not see the IT guy rushing past him until they had collided.

Dang, man, Ben thought as he assessed the situation. He could tell something was not quite right.

"Sorry, young man." He looked at Benjamin, remembering his face. "Did you ever get your laptop taken care of?"

"Yes, sir. I did. Thanks."

"Well, sorry again. I'm late to a meeting with the principal" he shook his head and closed his eyes. "I don't understand how someone breached our servers," he mumbled to himself, pinching the bridge of his nose. "Alright. See you later, kid."

Server breach. Ben shrugged his shoulders and carried on to class. The rest of his day seemed to almost crawl by from anticipation. Hanging out with others that were interested in similar topics as him and possessed if not the same but more knowledge, would be a breath of fresh air. School made him indifferent. Yes, the social aspect was nice; however, the course material seemed to lack something. Sometimes the topics were not interesting enough to keep his attention. The teachers were unprepared for curious minds and seemed to shy away from challenging students. Majority the teachers liked him because he caused no trouble, which allowed him the freedom to work on side projects or help other students with their work. Ben simply craved a challenge.

Ben's cheek rested in his palm as he propped his head up in his has last class when his phone vibrated in his pocket, signaling that he had a text message. *Dad is picking me up today?* His dad rarely picked him up so something was definitely suspicious from this morning. Classes were soon dismissed, and he made his way to the student pick-up area for his dad.

"Hey Dad!" Ben greeted when he reached the car. His dad bumped his fist and warmly embraced him.

"How was school, Benny boy?"

Looking out the window, Ben sighed. "It was okay. Went by kind of slow, though. I really was just ready for after school. You know you're taking me to the pizza place around the corner, right? I would've walked but mom insisted that I'm dropped off since it's my first time."

Darnell Smith gripped the steering wheel a little tighter at the mention of his wife. Things were shaky and the future of his family seemed uncertain. He loved them dearly, but things just seemed so hectic all of a sudden.

"Yeah, your mom told me. What is all this about anyways?"

"Well, just some kids that I met that are interested in computers and stuff. Nothing too unusual or anything." His dad nodded in approval as they arrived in front of the building. Through the store's front window, Ben could see a group of kids around his age sitting at a large table. "Well alright, Dad. This looks like my stop. Are you picking me up too?"

Ben's big brown questioning eyes made his dad hesitate. Darnell remembered the exact moment he felt pure love rush over him the first time he swaddled Benjamin close to his chest. He promised to never let anything or anyone hurt him yet he had no choice but to. "Yeah, I'll be picking you up. Text me when you're ready to go."

Ben nodded, hopping out of the car. Deep breaths filled his lungs to capacity as he attempted to calm his nerves. Although he wasn't a usually shy person, first encounters just got to him. His mind went into overthinking mode in an attempt to play out possible scenarios and how to be prepared for them. Sometimes, things don't go as planned. Walking in, the bell over the door alerted the restaurant of his presence. His eyes locked with the group and they welcomed him with inviting smiles. A boy wearing an orange Polo stood to greet him.

"Hey, you must be Big Bee Knee?" the table burst into joking giggles.

Ben chuckled himself in reflection about his username. "Yeah and you must be Super Mario Man?"

He nodded. "Yeah this is my dad's place, so we meet here every week or whenever something is going on. I'm Timothy and this is the group. We all know how it feels to be the new guy."

Ben instantly relaxed, no longer fearing that he would not be accepted. "Great, now I can breathe," he chuckled again. "I didn't know what to expect."

"Nah, we're pretty chill. Just pizza and geek stuff."

Geeks? But none of them look like geeks to me. Ben observed the table again for a closer inspection. Maybe he missed something. Not that it would matter but the tweens sitting around delicious smelling pizza and enjoying each other's company, all seemed normal. No extra thick glasses wrapped in tape or nasally correction floating amongst the room. Just regular kids wanting a good techy time. Ben finally felt at home as he sat around the table being introduced to the other members. He learned all about the group. Their name was the Tech Crew and had about 10 to 13 members when people had time to come. He got a chance to meet almost everyone from the random chat room that he wandered into and a few new people. Conversation flowed in all directions and people switched seats often when they went back up to get pizza. Tim's dad owned a pizza and dessert buffet. $5 gave them access to all the pizza, cinnamon buns and soda they could handle. Tim even offered them to-go boxes for later. Of course, Ben grabbed a few slices of Hawaiian for the road.

"So, has anyone gotten any info on the Crypt$$ey scandal that's going on right now?" A soft voice asked at the edge of the table. Ben leaned forward to glance down two seats over to see an brown skinned girl with onyx clouds for hair sitting to his right. His head tilted. He hadn't noticed her before.

"What's that?" he questioned, looking into her brown eyes. Something about her intrigued him.

She gave him a small grin. "You don't know about Crypt$$ey? It's the biggest thing going on right now. All this week it's been in the media. You don't have any social media?"

Ben glanced down, trying to recall any memory of passing the titles while he browsed online. But he was mainly focusing on school work. He guessed he hadn't been too deep in the tech underground after all. "No, not really. I'm kinda new to all this." he answered modestly. The two other kids between them got up to get more pizza, which allowed Ben to scoot down. "I'm Benjamin, by the way. I go to Harper Charter School," he introduced himself.

"Hey, I'm Fenty. I just moved here about a year ago

from Barbados with my mom. And I've never seen you at Harper before."

"Well unfortunately, I'm there quite a lot," they giggled.

"So what's the scandal about?"

"Well supposedly, this underground industry mogul that was investing in a lot of different things over the years and converted all of his money was into cryptocurrency. But he was just randomly killed like two days ago. And now hackers everywhere are trying to find his account," she explained.

"Wow, that's crazy. Why are they trying to find his account? What are they going to do when they get it?"

"They're going to steal it obviously."

He blinked wildly for a minute. *I wonder how.* Fenty noticed the confused look on his face and began teaching him the process of hacking and mining private cryptocurrencies. She knew so much that it blew Ben's mind. A boy from across the table overheard their conversation and joined in with Fenty.

"Yeah, it's a lot of money out there to be made all from the comfort of your desk. I'm Neyo, Fenty's big cousin," he said, introducing himself to Ben.

"Only by a year," Fenton rolled her eyes playfully.

"You just moved here or something? I've never seen you around these parts before." Neyo stuffed more pizza in his mouth and washed it down with orange soda.

"I'm Benjamin. And nah, my parents are just usually all over me. This is the first time they really just left me alone." He glanced down at his phone and noticed that neither his mom or dad had texted him. *That's definitely new.* Ben shrugged it off and continued his conversation. He was enjoying everyone's company. The energy mixed with the warm atmosphere made him feel at ease. He already couldn't wait until next week's meet up.

His dad finally texted him saying that he'd be out front in a few minutes. Ben gave his goodbyes to everyone and went outside to wait for his dad. With his hands in his pockets, Benjamin could feel something stirring in his spirit. The air felt different as it moved through his body. He couldn't put his finger on it, but life was changing. *I hope for the better.* A few seconds later, Mr. Smith arrived, gathered Ben and they were off towards home. Mr. Smith asked Ben about his time spent and was pleased to hear that he thoroughly enjoyed himself. He could see the joy in his eyes and the amusement in his voice as he recalled the events that he'd taken place. The light conversation was enough to last them until they got home. As they pulled into the driveway, the lights were off in the house.

"Hey son, your mom isn't feeling too well so try not to bother her too much."

"Do I ever?" Ben grinned at his dad. They shared a small chuckle knowing how Ben liked to be under his mom when they all were chilling together. Ben collected his belongings and followed his dad into the house. Silence was heavy and it felt unusual. He had never felt his home feel like that before. Shaking it off, Ben ran up to his room and closed the door. Usually, he'd hop on his computer to play around but it was getting late. He prepared for school by showering and picking his outfit out. Before he knew it, he was sound asleep.

However, his peaceful slumber did not last long. An itchy throat awoke him and left him in search of hydration. Usually, he'd have a water bottle on his nightstand between books and other knick-knacks, but he'd chugged the last one after the shower. Accepting the needed journey to the kitchen, Ben flung the fluffy black comforter off of his body and proceeded downstairs. Ben quickly raced downstairs against the darkness, snatched the refrigerator door, retrieved a bottle, and did a beeline for the door. Once at the top of the stairs, muffled yelling behind his parents' door caught his attention. His feet momentarily halted and then hesitated before allowing curiosity to pull him closer. *What would they be arguing about if mom was sick earlier?* It was rare to see his parents argue so he felt conflicted. He stood in front of the door illuminated by a dim light that glowed in the hallway. It was just enough to compete with the moon from the window and for him to notice the picture of the family on last Easter was missing. Only a shadow where it once was hung above the oil diffuser remained.

Benjamin could fully make out the words being exchanged, but he instead turned on his heels and returned to his room. Walking in, his hand rested on the door knob while his back collided with the door. He stood there taking in his room. The way his clothes and posters were assorted around the four walls. For some reason, he wanted to take inventory of his life. He wanted to relish in that current moment. At that moment, it was important for him to be able to close his eyes and mentally see his safe haven exactly the way he liked it; peaceful. Something in his gut said things were changing and fast. Pushing the thoughts out of his mind, he grabbed his laptop to distract him from what his chest was feeling. An hour had passed before the SandMan came to visit him.

The next day, he awoke to perform his daily routine. His

mom dropped him off at school and appeared to be pretty normal. The short hand on the clocks around him seemed to be dipped in molasses. Each class was long and filled with random noises that did not register to Ben. *Today must be an off day.* Ben shook his head as he wiped his palms over his face. He walked outside into the closed off courtyard that the building had in the center. The sun welcomed him and he began breathing on four counts. His mom had taught him breathing exercises for when his feelings felt too much to handle. But why was he feeling that way? Confusion rested on his chest and he was just ready to return home to play video games with his dad. He hoped a good battle in 2K would help him shake the weird feeling.

Around three-ish, the dismissal bell rang allowing the students to vacate the building. Ben checked his phone to see if he had gotten a message from his parents letting him know his ride home arrangements. To his surprise, neither one of them had contacted him. *Strange.* He tried calling them both and got no answer. He knew his house wasn't that far from his school so walking wouldn't be a problem. He just was unsure if his parents would agree. *Well, they ain't here.* He shrugged his shoulders and started his walk home. As he re-traced the route of the drive with his parents, he watched all the other kids go about their days. He imagined what their lives were like. Closer to the school were apartments and homes that had a bad reputation according to his parents and other students. There was hardly any upkeep on the homes and groups of people congregate in various spots along the streets. Some relaxed on their porches waving at the cars passing by and keeping an eye on the younger kids playing in scattered patches of grass. He caught eyes with some of the older guys standing on the corners. They nodded and he returned the gesture.

His mind then wandered to many places during his walk. So much so that he had arrived at his mailbox in no time. He observed the house noticing that his mom's car was parked in its usual spot. *Okay, now I definitely need to know what's up.* Benjamin tried practicing his breathing but found himself still getting upset. A loud commotion from the migration of geese caused him to look up. Dark, grey clouds sat above a pocket of blue skies and a plethora of cotton balls. He studied his eyes upon the window of sunshine and tried guessing how far the clouds traveled. Suddenly, the hairs on his left side tingled as he heard a stampede of some sorts. A curtain of water ambushed him as he darted to the door under the car port. Patting himself dry as he entered the kitchen, he saw the kitchen a complete mess. Chairs were overturned, copy papers all over the floor and the table shifted.

"Mom!" he called out. The house was dark and felt still.

"Huh?" he heard shuffling from upstairs. He walked towards the stairs to find his mom coming down. "I am so sorry baby," she cried, pulling him in for a close embrace. "I am so sorry, baby. I can't believe I left my baby. Oh my God!" she exclaimed, crumbling in his arms. He was now embracing her. All of her weight was resting on him as he looked down at his mother.

"Ma, where's Dad? What's wrong?" That only made her wails louder. The pain behind the sounds that erupted from her throat shocked him. He had never seen his mother so disheveled before. It was a strange and unusual sight.

After a few minutes, his mother finally composed herself. She used the back of her hand to remove the cocktail of liquids splattered across her face. Kimberly felt embarrassment in the pit of her stomach as she looked into her son's eyes. He was the reflection of a love that once was and she didn't have the heart to tell him. To tell him that she failed him. That she was not capable of keeping her family together. Ignoring that it takes two to tango, she took on full responsibility. Guilt wrapped around her tongue like hot iron, which prevented her to speak. To tell him how sorry she is. The differences could no longer be ignored and she had to step out on faith. For her. For Ben. For them.

"My Baby Bee," she cooed, holding the sides of his face. Memories of happier times in the past and lost futures flashed across her eyes. Tears clouded her vision again. With deep breaths, she steadied herself. "Things are going to be a little different from now on. Unfortunately, me and your dad just couldn't get things figured out. I know you're young, but I want to always tell you the truth. I love you and I will always love your father. I can never stop loving you guys. You guys are my world." *Deep breaths, girl. Pull it together.* "Your dad decided to move out. We are separating for some time. I don't know if or when he'll be back. You can talk to him for anything else. But please baby boy, just know that this is NOT your fault. You don't deserve this. This will not be your future. What me and your father have going on is between us."

A heavy silence hung in the air as Benjamin processed everything his mother had unloaded on him. This was a lot to take in at such a young age. Even though he had always been labeled as mature for his age, he was still just a kid at heart. The only two people he had ever known as a packaged deal would now be divided to live different lives. How would he even fit in the picture? What would life be like with each parent? So many questions swirled around his mind. He paused momentarily to look at the woman in front of him. He loved his mother. She was one of his best friends. They both were. They were the three musketeers. Now he felt like they had all broke apart. In that moment, he felt alone. But he couldn't show his mom that. She wouldn't be able to handle it right now.

Benjamin swallowed hard as he took his mother into his arms. He could taste the bitterness from his tears. They shared a long embrace, releasing their pain and sorrow. Together, they mourned and grieved the only life they had ever known. "I love you, Mom."

"I love you too, Benjamin. Please don't be mad at your father either. Sometimes things like this happen but everything will be alright. Some money stuff might get tight, but we can pull through, okay?"

He just nodded his head. They hugged one last time before parting ways into their designated rooms. They both had a lot to digest. When Ben entered his bedroom, his laptop was open and on.

`@CMurphy: Wanna make some fast cash?`

His left eyebrow slowly raised in suspicion. Ben knew for a fact he had it closed and turned off so it wouldn't burn out. But now how was his stuff up? He looked around the room and everything resembled his mental image. *What in the world is going on here?*

Chapter 3: Horizon

Large, puffy clouds drenched in dreary grey hues matched Benjamin's mood since he learned about his parents' new marital status. After fifteen years together, circumstances had caused for the couple to split, leaving Benjamin with more questions than answers. However, instead of the answers he wanted, he was met with isolation. His mom had taken on longer hours at work and his dad was across town. It was almost as if his parents were avoiding him.

Mornings were quiet. The evenings were cold. The nights were empty. Things in his home just didn't feel familiar anymore. Last week, Wednesdays had become his new favorite day. But today, he just wanted to stay home. No school. Just him and his thoughts. Ben sat on the edge of his bed with his toes dipping into the plush carpet. A heavy sigh escaped his lips. Unwillingly, he pulled himself together for school. *Maybe the pizza party will make something better.*

As Ben came down the stairs, he was surprised to see his mom still at home. Entering the kitchen, he remained silent with his hands balled into fist in his sweatpants' pockets. His breathing became slow and shallow. Seeing his mom slightly angered him while deep down, he knew he couldn't be mad at her. Or anybody else for that matter.

"Good morning Benjamin," Kimberly said, standing to embrace her son. Days seemed to blend into one another as each new hurdle appeared. It had been a long time since she had to live life without a partner. Parts of her routine changed. Work schedule. Eating habits. Sleeping pattern. Everything.

Ben stepped back a little, rejecting her affection. "Morning. I was just on my way out," he responded, curving around her towards the door.

"Oh, I can take you to school today," she said, watching him grip the door handle.

"I'm fine. I'm used to walking now. See you later," he said, closing the door.

It wasn't that he was mad at his mother but something black and itchy crawled into his chest each time he thought of either one of his parents. How could they *betray* him? His dad had not even attempted to contact him yet. But there he was, with just so many questions circling around his mind. How could he just be *okay* going from seeing Benjamin every day to radio silence? How was *his* father okay with that? How was his *mother* going to just abandon him? Too many mixed emotions flowed through his body which prompted him to briskly walk to school.

School started off uneventful as usual. Weird smells wafted through the air. Teachers yelled at students. Students argued back. He felt trapped in an intellectually suffocating environment that offered him limited happiness. Lunch was the only thing that mildly excited him because he could mess around on his laptop in the library. However, today made him want to explore the courtyard. There was a small sunroom for students to study in. Normally, it would be hard to find a free seat but there was a single seat next to two kids at a table. As Benjamin approached the long oak table, the faces of the students registered to him.

"Fenty? Neyo?" Ben called out to them. He had never

seen them around before. "So, this is where you guys been hiding."

Fenty lifted her head from her book and rolled her eyes playfully. "It looks like you finally found us," she said as Ben and Neyo slapped hands to briefly embrace.

"Scoot down," he lightly pushed Fenty's shoulder. Their eyes connected momentarily before they averted their gazes.

"Look, what ya' not finna do is put your hands on meh, boy," Fenty warned with laughter lacing her homeland accent.

"So, what brings you around to our parts? Somebody like you is normally where they're told," Neyo joked with Ben.

Benjamin shrugged his shoulders as he stuffed his hands in his jacket pockets, his leg bouncing quietly under the table. His heart still hurt from everything. Without looking up, he replied "I don't know. I just needed a new change of routine, I guess. What? Is that a crime?" He looked off into the distance, watching the students pass by. Fenty and Neyo caught on to his disposition.

"Change of routine, huh? Well, you know 'tis is the skippers' spot, right?" Fenty questioned him.

Skippers' spot? Ben focused his eyes back on Fenty. "Nah, I didn't know that. So, they just let y'all stay here all day? Who is even allowing this?" The group exploded with laughter from Ben's curiosity.

"Well, we stay here as long as we can. And then if we have to leave? Then well, we leave for good," Neyo and Fenty shared a giggle at his explanation.

"As in y'all just leave the school altogether?" Ben egged on for clarification.

Neyo's lips twisted upward as he examined Ben. "Yeah, boy. You wearing a wire or something?" he joked. "You're acting like you're working for the principal." They shared another round of laughter.

"Cuz, now that you mention it, this is his first time in here. He might be," Fenty poked her finger around his chest in playful searching.

"Get off me," Ben exclaimed in a dramatic harsh whisper. He popped Fenty's hands and shoved Neyo's shoulder. "Ya'll suck. I was just trying to figure out what was going on."

"Well yeah, that's what goes on here. We get away with it by being smart. You've already done all your work in the class. The teachers don't really have much else to do after that, so they let you go," Neyo explained. Ben shook his head in understanding. Indeed, all of his work had been completed for the week, so he was just going to be on his laptop during class.

"Okay, so let's go."

Fenty and Neyo stopped to see if Ben was serious. They could tell he was a little sheltered with a newfound freedom on the horizon. "Are you sure? You can't be all scared while you're with us."

Ben tooted his lips in offense. "Now y'all really think I'll be scared? I'm offended." He laid his hand over his chest. They all laughed at his theatrics.

"You ain't said nothing but a thang then," Fenty said as she and Neyo started packing their bags. Benjamin quickly followed suit. They were professionals at skipping school. They never got into any real trouble, but school was just so boring. They had better stuff they could be doing than to be sitting in a stuffy, uncomfortable room all day. They were more productive in spaces that promote individuality and tranquility. Not stifling and stanky.

The trio nonchalantly exited the sunroom and headed in the direction towards the back of the school near the ramp where the bus loaded and unloaded. There were four train tracks that separated the school property line and the rest of the city. Across the train tracks were restaurants, the metro train station and other little shopping stores.

This is NOT the move, Ben thought. He wouldn't dare say it aloud for the others to hear, though. They already thought he was a baby, no reason to add delicate to the list. Tiny rocks scratched at Ben's ankles as they climbed the small hill to the metal tracks. The sun was directly over them as they made their journey to an unknown location. Ben's foot slipped on the rocks, causing him to slide backwards. Regaining his posture, he jogged to the top and hopped over the tracks to rejoin his group.

"So y'all wasn't going to wait on me?" Ben interrogated, slightly out of breath. They just laughed at him and started walking toward the metro station. The walk went by fast as the trio discussed possible lounging locations. They settled on a smoothie cafe that Fenty said had "chill vibes". She had an extra metro pass that Ben could borrow so they could get to their destination. Fenty and Neyo were not new to public transportation; however, Benjamin had been chauffeured his whole life. Close eyes would be kept on him to make sure he didn't get swept up in the hustle and bustle of the inner-city flow.

Catching the train downtown went a lot smoother than Ben expected. The passengers didn't seem to pay attention to the young teens, which gave Ben some relief. He was nervous. He had never disobeyed his parents to this extent.

A few white lies here and there, but never skipping school. *What if my parents found out?* Then it dawned on him. They were out of the picture now. He now had endless possibilities of what *he* wanted to do. If his parents wanted space, then he deserved some too. His whole life, they had joint control over every single detail. Some that he didn't agree with. But now with them occupied with their own lives, he had time to do the same. Benjamin took a deep inhale as the escalator dropped him off in the middle of downtown. He had never been without his parents and the air had a strong stench of liberation amongst other weird things. With their bookbags gripped tightly to their backs, they blended into the crowd of city-goers. There was pushing, many excuse-me's, odd stares, random smells, and other events that stimulated his senses. The experience was invigorating, and they hadn't even done anything yet.

Fenty led them into her favorite hideaway spot. The atmosphere had a very different vibe from the pizza parlor. It felt way more mature. The walls were old red bricks and lights hung low over the tables. There weren't many people which made it even better. They settled in the lounge area that had accent chairs, a fur rug, and ottomans to use as foot rests.

"Time to set up shop," Neyo said as he pulled out his laptop.

"Have y'all gotten that 'Fast cash' message online?" Ben asked, remembering the weird occurrence.

"Yeah. I heard it's legit, but please be aware of what can happen on the Dark web. You can run into a lot of messed up people," Neyo warned. "Folks can really deceive you online."

"Messed up people? Like what? I need some examples."

"Well, I heard about this one kid that had started doing some work for somebody and they wanted to stop. Whoever it was didn't like that. The following day, the kid started seeing cars pull into their driveway at night and just sit for hours. Then they'd randomly leave. There's even a video posted somewhere of them opening up a box and on the inside was an open bag labeled 'Contaminated Waste'. After that, they never logged back on again."

"Can I see the video?"

"Already on it," Fenty said, sliding him her computer. They sat in silence, watching the kid a little older than them search the contents of the box, scream and then frantic ending of the video.

They sat there for a second, thinking. "Well, what if the video is fake? He could've just made another account," Ben reasoned. He had never been one to easily believe fables.

"Well look, if you want to try it. Go ahead. But at least do it smartly and not like ole boy here," Fenty said pointing at the screen. "Are you using a VPN and virtual machine?"

"Uh no. What are any of those things?"

Neyo and Fenty shared side eyes with each other. "So, you telling me you've been on Tor using your regular machine and addresses?"

"Uh yeah. I wasn't doing too much so I didn't think anything of it. Was that a bad idea?"

They shook their heads at Ben's ignorance. They couldn't blame him though. He was just learning and a baby in their deep techno world. The majority of his lessons would have to come through trial and error, but they wanted to set him up with the basics first. An hour had passed while they explained to Ben what a virtual private network is, how to set up a bitcoin account for untraceable currencies, using a virtual machine for a buffer between his sensitive information and potential threats, how to conduct business virtually, and so much other stuff. The group was huddled around Ben's computer as they communicated back and forth with FastCash Guy, trying to negotiate his deal. FastCash wanted Ben to test a few interfaces out for him. He would be sending Ben a list of websites and apps for him to give feedback on and in return he would get 10 bitcoins. When Fenty and Neyo informed Ben that bitcoins were actually worth more than the US dollar, the deal was sealed. He knew asking his parents for stuff would be difficult now, so he needed a way to support himself. In his mind, he'd just hit the jackpot.

"Where can I cash out these bitcoins?"

"Save them to a flash drive and take them to a professional. But most people just keep them and buy stuff on the web with them. You're not really supposed to make them into liquid cash," Neyo informed. Ben shook his head as he started devising his plan.

"Wait. You aren't saving any of this on your computer, are you?" Fenty asked, raising an eyebrow.

"Nah. I found some server with some free space."

"Uh what? You don't even know where this stuff is being sent and stored?" Fenty shook her head. She snatched Ben's laptop. Her fingers became a blur as she began retracing Ben's digital footprint. She located his data's address and did a GPS scan to see an exact location of the server. Her mouth hung open in disbelief.

"What?" Both Neyo and Ben said in unison. She turned the laptop around to reveal that the location was their school.

"Boy, you better backup all your stuff right now on this

drive," Fenty instructed, passing Ben a spare drive. "You have just been living life so reckless. I'm glad you met us," she said, giggling.

Ben joined her. "How was I supposed to know? But this does make sense now. The IT guy had said something about a server breach."

"I wouldn't trust our school's IT team to guard a dirty sock, okay? They don't know no more than you do," Neyo joked at Ben.

"Man whatever. I'm going to buy an external hard drive with this 'fast cash' so I don't have to worry about this anymore."

"We hope so."

The crew stayed at the coffee shop for another couple of hours before getting antsy. They packed up their belongings and ventured back out into the concrete jungle. Ben followed closely behind Fenty as he digested his surroundings. The shiny skyscrapers glistened in the sun. Large intersections allowed pedestrian traffic to bustle amongst the cars. They quickly crossed several blocks before arriving at a familiar looking park. There was a fountain centerpiece that allowed free play. Classical music played lightly in the background as water shot up through the spots in the ground. Multicolored lights joined in the tango and made a beautiful performance. There were other statues around the enclosed area. In the distance, Ben could see some of the city's tourist attractions. They made their way down to a secluded area hidden by low hanging branches. Large boulders sat alongside a babbling brook.

Benjamin became quiet as his memory began to play in front of his eyes. He remembered coming here a few years ago with his parents. It was the Fourth of July celebration.

He could hear fireworks and laughter. Phantom smells of BBQ and sweets floated through the air. Warm feelings overtook his body as he saw his parents smile and kiss under the night sky as he sat on his dad's shoulder.

You better not cry, Ben thought, trying to suppress his emotions.

"Ben, are you okay?" Fenty asked, noticing his disposition again. She didn't want to pry earlier, but now she could fully tell that something was bothering him. "Talk to us. We're your buddies now."

He licked his lips and tucked his bottom one tightly in between his teeth. He didn't want to say everything out loud in fear that it might hurt too much. That it will be real. But he couldn't keep holding it in. He desperately wanted to confide in somebody. He looked into the eyes of his new companions and decided who better than them.

Fenty and Neyo leaned closer towards him in anticipation. He took in a deep breath. "My dad left us last night," he said, barely above a whisper.

Their faces went blank. They remembered his dad coming to pick him up at the pizza parlor the other day. Ben had spoken so highly of his father. But now the thought of him was bringing tears to his eyes. Their lack of experience handling sensitive matters had them tongue tied. How do you console a friend that has lost the only life he has ever known? He wasn't like them. They never really had too much of a parental relationship with either of their parents, so this was unknown territory.

"I'm so sorry, Benjamin. I wish there was something we could do," Fenty offered, laying her head on his shoulder. She lightly rubbed his back as he continued to cry. He felt so weak. So embarrassed.

Neyo rested his hand on Ben's other shoulder. "If it makes you feel any better, me and Fenty never met our dads. They left before we were born. So just be happy that you had time with him."

"But he's not returning any of my calls."

Neyo and Fenty made sour faces at each other. That was never a good sign. "Maybe he's hurt too. Just because he's an adult doesn't mean he doesn't make mistakes or hurt too. But what happened to you was wrong and it was not your fault," Fenty offered.

Ben remained silent. He didn't care. His dad had never treated him like this before. So, what was making him do it now? Every time Ben thought about his dad, anger and questioning were the only things he felt.

"He abandoned me and my mom. You should see her. She's just not the same anymore," Ben's chin rested on his chest as more tears fell. "I'm sorry y'all."

"No need to apologize to us. It makes complete sense to feel that way. Everybody cries. Everybody feels pain once or twice in their lives," Fenty said, trying to comfort him. "I know for a fact that Neyo cries in the shower on Thursdays."

They all burst into small chuckles. "Yeah, that's only cause Fenty reveals her real ugly face on those nights," he retorted in his defense.

Looking up, they could see various shades of pink and purple painted on the horizon. The sun was getting ready to make its exit and the group decided it was time to head home. Cars had abandoned the asphalt to rest. Tired masks from social interactions were ready to be hung by entry ways. Stomachs growled in need of fuel for recharging. Fenty and Neyo's apartment was in the opposite direction of his home so they said their goodbyes and went to their respective paths. Ben departed with his heart less heavy and his mind a little more full.

Chapter 4: Set Up

New York, New York

175 blurs of blue, black and grey suits of fine cottons, silks and velvets adorning the bodies of important shareholders, chief executive officers and chief financial officers all escaped the historic skyscraper. Top companies from all over the world were invited to meet and mingle on an agenda for the upcoming market launches. It was a day filled with gourmet delectables and hushed whispers from the elite in grand halls floating above the city. Recollections of the many benefits of selected generational wealth was exchanged amongst the attendees while discussions of strategic business advancements were tangled in between. It was a private gathering until the law required the group to disclose an abbreviated draft for the public. All the silent handshakes over well written, air-tight contracts would not make the cut. No, those were typed and locked away in the memory boards of hired reporters of each company.

Kathy Campbell waited curbside for the valet to flag down a taxi for her and her assistant. Looking at her fresh set of nails, she hopped into the backseat once the vehicle arrived. "I need you to read to me the important notes, please. I was so terribly tired in that meeting that I couldn't even pay attention." She grabbed the designer shades from her handbag and rested her head back on the seat. Melany began reciting the confidential information for her boss. This was not an unfamiliar task to her. For the past three years, Kathy Campbell had been running in the shoes of her mother to manage an inherited bio-tech company. She, like many others, were perfect targets to leech vulnerable information from.

Forty-five minutes later, they arrived at their hotel. Melany glanced down at the chaos erupting on her mobile screen. Messages upon messages vibrated from various contacts of not only hers, but Kathy's as well. "Um, Kathy, you may want to brace yourself to look at this."

Melany handed her boss the phone with her stomach in knots. Kathy's eyes swelled with tears as she saw private emails, messages, pictures, documents and other revealing data plastered all over the web. "What. Is. Going. On!" she screamed at the entrance of the hotel.

Seeing the commotion Kathy was about to start, Melany quickly escorted her to the suit. Kathy's personal phone began ringing, signaling she had a specific caller. Kathy and Melany locked eyes, knowing who it was.

"Hello William. What do I owe the pleasure of this call?" Kathy's stomach was flipping.

"Let's skip the pleasantries, my dear, because I'm sure you know the reason why I'm calling," William, head of security, stated. "The company is currently sinking from leaked information. It seems as though you and a few others' devices have been compromised. We did a remote scan of your computer and found several active worms from unknown locations. After examining them, they'd been scanning your conversations and system for keywords. I'm almost positive all of the phones with you have been tapped as well." Kathy and Melany both thought back to the random link sent to their text messages and felt nauseous.

"So well after that meeting," he sighed, "things just ran

wild. That being said, you need to get back here immediately. There is a press conference on the way." And with that, he hung up. Kathy and Melany sat on the floor with heavy heads as they came to grips with their hacking.

Silicon Valley, California

"Hey Phil, catch!" Tyler exclaimed, tossing the foam football at his coworker. TraeTech, one of the modern world's most popular online trading companies, promoted open workspaces for a laidback environment. Phil, the lead software engineer, caught the ball before it knocked over the stack of printed code on his desk.

"Tyler, stop messing around and get back to work," he reprimanded, throwing it back. Before Phil could sit down, a loud power zap snapped through the air. The room was silent with only the windows to provide lighting. Instinctively, everyone pulled their phones' flashlights out. Within seconds, the power was reconnected. However, the computers of several employees displayed bright, green characters against an onyx background while others were frozen on a green screen. Commotion erupted from the building as the realization sunk in. Seconds passed like fresh paint drying on a wall. "We've been compromised! We've been hacked!" was shouted in all directions as panic took over. They all started closing laptops and trying to disable the power off function, but were unable to completely shut off. It was possible that even in sleep mode, the attack would still be executing.

"Check the app and website from your phone!" Phil shouted, standing on his desk. They were all greeted with an Error 404 message. "They're DDoS'ing us too!" Phil slammed his fist into the ceiling. He knew this could cost the company millions and ultimately, he'd be responsible for it all. Tight security on a well-oiled machine was his one duty, and at that moment, nothing represented succeeding.

After experiencing several minutes of chaos, some employees opted out of the hot mess express whereas others sat close to the dumpster fire, bathing in its glory. They all knew the company was now in a hole. Quiet stares were shot at Phil and Tyler. They were the leaders so the team couldn't possibly be blamed.

Tyler slowly strolled to Phil's desk and stood there a moment, holding his "World's Best Coder" mug. "You know we're screwed right?" Tyler waited for a response. Receiving nothing, he continued. "Well, who dunit? Somebody inside here would have been in the know".

Phil glanced up at Tyler through his wire-frame glasses. Tyler had always seemed like a little brother to him. He was a younger frat brother from college that he was just trying to help out. Nothing like this would have ever happened before. Upset at himself, Phil just shook his head, returning to the screen. He watched the computer shutdown. He stared at it suspiciously as it went through its usual boot up routine.

"Check the balances," Tyler urged.

Phil squinted his eyes at Tyler, but remained silent. He too was curious of the loss. *How skilled were these intruders?*

A large gasp escaped his throat, trying to calm his now irregular breathing. He stared at the bright, red negative numbers that estimated close to 5.6 million dollars. Seeing his reaction, Tyler circled around the desk to see and shared in his astonishment. Phil ran all ten fingers through his dark brown hair.

"Hey, if Timothy comes in here, you talk to him." Phil patted Tyler on the shoulder. He grabbed his important belongings with whatever else could fit in his book bag and looked around one last time before exiting. He'd be leaving with some dignity, not because he was dragged out by the ankles for being the world's biggest idiot.

Somewhere on the Dark Web

The phrase "I hope everyone got their moneyyy," floated over the network with laughter erupting soon after. Each hacker from their respective country was assigned an account. With this account, they had one mission: drain it dry. No one knew any one's identity, but had built a trust to hit cyber heist together. It wasn't that they couldn't meet up. Over the last year, @CMurphy has allowed plenty of funds for a flight. However, it was protection. No face, no case. However, they were willing to disclose their username and homeland. That was their only trace, if it was even true. There were five members under the age of 27.

@nadiii: Female from Russia, 18.

@abeo: Male from Nigeria, 24.

@aLthat: Female from China, 17.

@makonnen: Male from United States, 21.

@oliey: Female from Romania, 26.

Their intelligence was deliberately selected by @CMurphy. Each one possessed a special skill that helped him carry out various attacks. @CMurphy delivered the mark folder and they carried out the assignments in exchange for 90% of the profit. It was almost too good to be true. By hijacking private information, the team was able to collect $578,000 each. They used the stolen meeting data to influence the market of those companies. They hacked their accounts, selling their stocks to inside traders. Money gathered from sales was quickly converted into bitcoins and stored into their many servers. The entire operation took less than ten minutes to execute and two months of planning. But the payoff was always worth the time.

"I have to go now. I'll be around if we get another folder," @abeo added before disconnecting.

"He's always so warm," @oliey commented. She giggled before continuing. "Well, goodbye team and until next time." They all disconnected and went on to live their real lives.

The temperature in the sunroom was comfortable and inviting to the students as they spent their last block hiding away. They had all been spending more time with each other working for @CMurphy testing the strength of particular websites. It was shared that it was helping a contracting company do user studies. The awarded funds could be traded for various gift cards, which allowed them to buy whatever they wanted. In just a week, they had acquired a nice lump sum. @CMurphywas cool so far. He worked in social software in Europe. He was never late on assignments or payments, which made him a stand-up guy to the group.

"So I know y'all hadn't heard about what happened to TraeTech." Neyo said, glancing up from his laptop. Fenty rolled her eyes because regardless of how they responded, Neyo had to tell his stories. Ben just raised his eyebrows in anticipation. "Well, word on the web is that some hackers got together and shut them down. And they were the ones responsible for that data leak from all those companies."

"Didn't that all happen in the same day?" Fenty quizzed, because she too had heard of the latest gossip.

"Yup! Man, whoever did that, hit the jackpot. I just know they all got hundreds of thousands of dollars. The company lost close to five million dollars," Neyo added.

"You think that was an inside job?" Ben questioned, tuning in.

"Had to be. How else would they just supernaturally know how to time all that?"

Fenty tilted her head back in thought. "You think they used like an army of bots and stuff? I'm sure you'd have to have like a computer farm."

"Whatever they had, it got them rich," Neyo said, with a sigh. The group became quiet as thoughts about their separate desires consumed them, each feeling that problems could be solved with a financial increase.

Benjamin's laptop made a small chirping sound, signaling that he had a message via the alternate system that Neyo and Fenty installed. Switching to that desktop, he opened it, recognizing the username.

```
@CMurphy: @BigBeeKnee I have been
greatly appreciative of your
assistance. You show much potential
for greater challenges. If you are
willing, I would like for you to
complete an impossible task. You
will be given a folder with the
information to an associate of
mine. He has volunteered his
account to see if you would succeed
```

```
in retrieving several of his
passwords from his personal
computer. As always, the reward
will be well worth it.
```

The too perfectly timed message had shocked the group. Their minds buzzed because the task was not difficult, but trusting the unknown was. They were unsure that the message was completely true. Not too many people would be willing to just hand over their vulnerabilities. They wanted to be suspicious, but the urge to be financially secure quieted all alarms. Contemplation sat on each of the teens' chests. Before Ben could respond, his phone vibrated.

"Y'all, my dad is outside. I'll be right back," Ben stood to his feet to depart. He hadn't heard from his dad and was not about to miss a chance to talk to him. Yes, he was mad, but he loved his hero.

"Wait! What are you going to do about C. Murphy?" Fenty called out behind him.

Ben did not respond as he walked towards his father's designated pick-up spot. Seeing his car, he pulled the front passenger handle and jumped in. A moment passed as they took in the sight of each other. They soon embraced, holding each other for old times' sake. There was no way Ben could stay mad at his inspiration. Having a positive male role model in his life helped show him right from wrong when confusion clouded his vision. As much as the small fire burned in Ben's chest about how his dad had recently treated him, the love in his heart wouldn't allow him to deny this visit out of spite. Maybe he needed to cherish the times more?

"I'm so sorry son," Mr. Smith said, gripping the back of Ben's head, just to feel his tight coils. He remembered holding him as a baby where all of him fit in his palm. "I know I've been absent. I'm sorry. I messed up. I honestly don't know what's going on right now and I can't let you see me like that. As a person, it hurts not just your heart, but ego as well to not have an answer for your child. I have no answer for your questions because I don't know. Just know that regardless, I love you. Give me some time to figure things out."

"Is that what you told Mom too?"

Mr. Smith was silent as his son's question sat in. "Yes, that is what I told your mom too."

"Did you cheat on her? What happened? You don't want to be with us anymore or something, Dad?"

"Ben-"

"No. I'm not a kid anymore. I deserve to know as well."

"Benjamin, I don't know. I feel restless. I want to experience life. No matter what son, go experience life. I've been here my whole life working and doing less living. I told your mom, but she's afraid. So I couldn't wait. It sounds selfish," he shrugged, looking down. "But go living and you'll understand."

Ben sat there, examining and sorting his thoughts and feelings. What little freedom he had recently experienced was indeed addicting. He couldn't put his finger on it, but his dad gave them words. His father's honesty and bluntness would always hold his respect. He taught him how to respect, even when the truth was too honest or not agreeable. So why should now be any different?

"I guess, Dad. I'm still hurt. I'm not over everything. All this is crazy. I barely see Ma. It's just me. And it's like you left me. You could have at least taken me with you." Ben could feel his hurt and frustration surfacing. Yes, it made logical sense, but his heart still ached. He *wanted* both parents.

"Ben, you know I'll always be there for you. But that's why I needed to see you. My job offered me a position across the country and I'm taking it."

The car got silent as Ben connected all the dots. He nodded his head. It did not matter what he said because his dad was going to take the job. Part of him broke inside. There was a time when he thought his dad was an angelic figure. He had no flaws. Pure as snow. But now he saw him for him. A person just trying to figure life out too. It would be selfish of him to make him stay.

"Fine, Dad. I'm happy for you. Is that what you want me to say because I'm not. It's whatever," Ben shrugged. Pain was evident in his voice, but he refused to cry anymore over the situation. There was absolutely nothing he could do at that point besides live his life. *I wonder, would things ever feel the same?*

Mr. Smith nodded, understanding his son's response. That was expected. He taught Ben to always speak his mind with him. The world will chew you up if you don't. "Well, that's fine. I still love you. We can still video chat. You can come visit. Maybe hopefully bring your mom along."

"Are y'all really getting a divorce?" Ben turned to look his father in the eyes.

"I don't know, Benny. She said she's sending papers, so I guess we'll just have to wait and see. I still love your mother and always will. There's nothing in the world that's going to stop me from loving my family."

Ben could hear the love there from previous times when his father stated that. Part of him relaxed. Maybe his parents were just going through something. *Things can turn around.*

"Well, you can make some of this up to me by taking me to get some tacos," Ben said, side eyeing Mr. Smith once he pulled out the parking lot.

"Now you know I can hook my boy up with some tacos. Joes To Go?"

"Joes To Go," Ben responded, feeling like old times. For a moment in time, everything was fine.

A few hours later, Benjamin was dropped off with a full belly and a new game for them to play online. Running upstairs to his sanctuary, he bypassed all the darkness downstairs. He knew in about an hour or so, his mom would be coming home. *Let's see if these losers are online.*

Ben kicked off his shoes, plopped down on his bed and popped open his laptop. The message from @CMurphy was still displayed. Switching to his previous desktop, he hit messaged their group chat.

> **@BigBeeKnee:** hey where yall at?
> **@fynT:** home. wassup?
> **@BigBeeKnee:** i want to do that "impossible task" lol. I already got the folder and everything
> **@neeeyooo:** Oooooohhhhhh Big Ben yall!! what made you wanna do it?
> **@BigBeeKnee:** i just gotta live life.
> **@fynT:** seriously? thats your final answer?

@**BigBeeKnee**: yeah, why wouldnt it be?

@**fynT**: oh idk im just making sure. if you like it, then i love it.

@**neeeyooo**: shes mad lmbo

@**BigBeeKnee**: but for whyyy tho

@**neeeyooo**: no clue

@**fynT**: not really. dont care. so you know how you gon do it?

@**BigBeeKnee**: Was kinda hoping that yall would help. You know im going to split everything. Team work make the dream work XD !!!

@**fynT**: oh hes really laying it on thick today. Hes in a good mood lol

@**neeeyooo**: You talk with your dad went good bruh?

@**BigBeeKnee**: Yeah, we talked. We got tacos and a new game. im good.

@**fynT**: Crybaby!! Lmbo!

@**BigBeeKnee**: HEY!

@**fynT**: jkjk jk jk stop being so sensitive. its all love.

@**BigBeeKnee**: better be.

@**neeeyooo**:okay yall so how we gon do this?

@**fynT**: Brb i might have a buffer overflow code in my files somewhere

@**neeeyooo**: Why would you even have that???

@**fynT**: Hey. this is a judgment free zone, remember sir

@**neeeyooo**: yeah i guess lol

@fynT: Attachment 1: BuffAny3.c
@fynT: Run it how we showed you with the VM
@BigBeeKnee: bet. hold on

Within seconds, Ben was remotely locked into the client's computer. The "Big Payback" blasted in the background. Listening to music that his parents played during his earlier years helped him to focus. He hijacked the camera using a code he found online to make sure he was alone. He navigated to web browsers and injected the code into the background. Instantly, he had a folder self-generated with files upon files of information from the cookies and soft memory. Benjamin's eyes lit up. He had never seen anything like that before. These are some cool kids.

@neeeyooo: You good boy?
@BigBeeKnee: Yeah, my bad. I went to get a water lol. But yea i got everything. I'm about to send it to him now.

Minutes ticked by as they awaited his response. Ben heard his phone vibrate next to the mouse of his computer.

@CMurphy has sent you **$5,500** for **Impossible Tasks.**

Ben sent both Fenty and Neyo $1800 for their help.

@BigBeeKnee: I like this yall XD

Chapter 5: School Blues

Monday

The bell for the fourth block announced that class would begin in three minutes. Getting caught in the late bell meant detention for the rest of the day. Automatically sent to the gym. Benjamin quickly sat down in his assigned seat and pulled out his phone. *Skip 4th block and meet at the station?* Ben side eyed the door of his biology class taught by Coach Freeman. Fenty had messaged the group and as usual, wanted to leave. He shrugged his shoulders, ready for whatever.

Sliding out the side of the door against the flow of traffic, he sped walked directly up the halls. The back halls of the buildings were only for science classes and sported bare, white walls lacking lockers. His feet instinctively made a sharp right up the ramp, connecting to the middle of the building. The gym and cafeteria sat next to each other in the main hall. Ben gave short glances over both shoulders as he pushed against the metal door to the south campus parking lot. There was a gate with a chain, that if loose enough, one could slide through it to the other side or else risk getting caught by jumping over it. He walked closer to the gate to examine it. *Locked.* Glancing over his shoulder again, he slid his book bag through the small opening at the bottom. Steadily, he placed his right foot on the center of the chain as he pulled himself up and over the gate. As he came down, the gold necklace his parents got him snapped from the exposed wire. *Dang it!*

A feeling of him being watched came over him, causing

Ben to look up at the field. A tall figure was there in the distance, hidden in the shadows. The figure stepped closer into the sun. *Coach Freeman?* Benjamin's breath caught in his throat as his stomach sank. *Aww, snap.* Refusing to return, he made eye contact with Coach Freeman as he lifted his chin up and down in his direction. Coach returned the gesture. The stare down ended with Ben running up the street, away from the building. The feeling of paranoia kept sneaking up on him in fear that the Coach had sent the school's officers after him. When he finally reached the train station, he was relieved to see his crew.

"Finally," Fenty greeted once he came into her sight. "It feels like we've been waiting forever for you, boy." She smiled at him, waiting for a smart remark. Ben slapped hands with Neyo and gave Fenty a playful shove with his shoulder.

"Well, Coach Freeman caught me leaving out," Ben revealed.

"You didn't get in trouble?" Fenty shot at him.

"You ain't get followed, did you?" Neyo added, looking around him. Now everyone was on edge.

"Nah, I don't think so. We just kind of stared at each other. I nodded. He nodded. Then I ran off."

"Wow, so you just had a western showdown with the main teacher that we all have an interaction with? Okay," Fenty nodded. "Not very smart if you ask me, Benny."

Ben eyed Fenty suspiciously. She had never referred to him as Benny before. "Either way, the train is coming. Let's just get out of here," Neyo interjected. They grabbed their bags closer to their bodies as they faced the crowd to get on the train towards downtown.

The train arrived soon after, whisking them away to their

hideout cafe. Making money with C. Murphy had been their steady hustle over the last several months. Any odd job he requested, they figured it out and got it done. No questions were asked, only answers about payments. The crew enjoyed their time together crawling through the web. Ben had become another cousin they didn't know they needed. Neyo and Fenty provided the companionship of siblings that Ben always wanted.

"So, there's a hackathon coming up in a few weeks. I think we should enter. We don't really have any competition as far as I'm concerned," Neyo stated, stretching his arms out. His body relaxed in a plush, beanbag chair. Fenty sat across from him in a navy-blue accent chair. Ben, in the middle of the conversation, raised his head from his computer. He reflected on Neyo's words. *We would be undefeatable.*

"What's the prize?" Fenty's eyebrow shot up.

"A three-day trip to Disney World for *all* the winners."

Silence came over the group as thoughts of childhood dreams coming true settled in their hearts. Usually, Fenty and Neyo wouldn't entertain such thoughts but with Ben, came a breath of fresh air. New possibilities seemed to find them wherever they went when he was around. They both had to grow up earlier than expected due to absent parents and support structure. But when they were all together, they didn't feel the weight of the world on their shoulders. Just fun.

"I say we go for it. I always wanted to go," Ben said. His parents had made many promises to take him, but the day just never came. Images of him and his buddies running through the park filled his mind.

"Yeah, let's sign up tomorrow so we can go to the

happiest place on earth," Fenty joked. They all laughed, but deep down, hoped they would win. They finished a few more assignments for C. Murphy and left the shop. Their heads were a little higher with hopes of possible fun and excitement.

Wednesday

"Uh Mr. Smith, may I speak with you for a second," Coach Freeman whispered to Benjamin as he entered the classroom doorway. Ben looked up to meet various pairs of eyes. Backtracking his steps, he turned on his heels to exit.

"How are you doing today, Coach Freeman?" Ben greeted, sticking his hands in his jacket pockets.

"Why'd you skip my class on Monday?" he responded, folding his arms across his chest.

Silence was Ben's only response. He held his gaze with an emotionless face. *Why say too much and incriminate myself?*

"So, you don't have anything to say for yourself?"

Silence. Coach Freeman inspected the young man's demeanor. He was nonchalant about the issue and showed no remorse. He couldn't completely read him.

"Look Benjamin, a few of your teachers and I have noticed a change in your behavior. I rather speak to you first before calling home. What you did is indeed punishable by law. But I don't want to take it that far. None of us do. However, we are not permitting you to participate in the hackathon. This-"

"What?" Benjamin blurted out, taken aback. His face twisted into a disgusted ball. "How does that even make sense?"

"It doesn't have to make sense. We are the adults. You

don't get to have fun when you skip school."

Ben just looked off to the side because he knew he was wrong. "So, you're being serious right now, Coach?"

"Yes Benjamin. I am," he responded, sticking his chest out.

Ben scanned the man in front of him from head to toe and back up again. "Okay," he shrugged. "Are you ready to start class, sir?"

Coach Freeman eyed Ben suspiciously. This attitude was not like the Ben from a few months earlier. No. This new one was a little bolder. "After you, son."

Benjamin smirked. Nodding his head, he turned towards the door. "Thanks, sir."

For the rest of the class, he sat in his seat, fuming. His head shifted between his palms as he tried to rebuke the negative thoughts and feelings that consumed him. There was an itchy, burning sensation in his chest that wouldn't allow him to focus. His eyes scanned the classroom as he examined his peers and surroundings. The painted cinder block walls and melancholic faces only fueled his despair. Part of him understood that his actions had consequences. *I just ain't think it'd be this.* However, a good majority of him felt as though Coach Freeman was blowing things out of proportion. The hackathon was supposed to be a ticket to his happiness. A new environment to create lifelong bonds with his new friends. A trip to Disney World would replace all of the tragedy that happened this school year. Now it felt as if the dust of Disney was slipping through his fingers.

The dismissal bell alerted everyone that school was over. The students gathered their belongings, knocked off the grit of confinement, and headed in their respective destinations. Ben walked alongside Fenty and Neyo as they walked home. Benjamin wanted to enjoy his friends and their antics, but the news from earlier weighed him down. Sharing that information with them would bring down the mood.

"Ben, you good? You've awfully quiet," Fenty commented. She took a glance over at him to see his head down and hands in his pockets.

"Yeah, usually, you would've had something smart to say," Neyo added.

"Nah, I'm good, y'all. I'm just tired. It's been a looong day," Ben stated, brushing them off. As badly as he wanted to share, he just couldn't. *Maybe Coach was just bluffing.*

"If you say so. You know where to find us if you need us," Fenty said, stopping at their apartment complex. "Are you getting online tonight? Murphy sent us an assignment."

"Probably so. I just want to lie down for a while and then I'll log on."

"Cool." They all slapped hands and embraced before Fenty and Neyo disappeared into their home.

Ben continued his walk home. His spirit was so crushed that listening to his favorite tunes wouldn't raise them. The sound coming from headphones seemed more like an annoyance than comforting. Walking to nature's melodies, nearby birds flew above his head like racing planes. He entered the dark house and went to his room. There, he crashed on his bed, sulking. He had no idea what to do. He didn't want to tell his friends in fear that they'd blame him. He couldn't risk losing his new family.

"Forget Coach Freeman. I'm still going to enter and win," Benjamin said out loud as he logged on to join the crew. He was not fond of the sour feelings resting in his spirit. "I'll just do what I have to do," he shrugged, pushing thoughts of today's events to the back of his mind. *Now to the tasks at hand.* He popped his knuckles before typing away, lost in the dark web.

Monday

Today's the day. Just breathe and act normal. If they let you in? Cool. If not? Well, we'll just see. Benjamin had to give himself a pep talk as he walked towards the gym. His palms were sweaty, and his stomach did small flips. Being nervous was an understatement. He did not doubt his or his team's computing abilities, but he was aware of an uncertain threat. The last several weeks left Benjamin introverted and withdrawn at school. None of his teachers cared to ask why, but judged in the privacy of their lounge. Luckily for him, they weren't attending the event.

The hackathon would be a two-hour competition against four other teams after school. A Hack for Good is what the organizers named it. It was a nice farewell gesture to the students to celebrate the closing of a school year. Thick black curtains were positioned into squares to provide an illusion of isolation for the teams. The goal was to defend their computational ecosystem against attacks from their opponents. Many systems would be vulnerable, including two computers, routers, and other access points. Finger sandwiches, diced fruit, chips and various beverages were provided as light refreshments near the judges' table. A small stage was assembled with a projector and screen to display the remaining time.

Benjamin stood at the entrance, contemplating his decision. Two large red doors separated him from the commotion taking place inside. Through the glass, he could see the participants getting situated. Cold air filled his lungs as the metal handle rested in his hand. *Let's do this.*

"Ready to win?" Neyo greeted Ben as he approached their assigned section. They slapped hands and embraced each other.

"Of course." Ben looked around at their competition as they scurried around. "I think this is going to be an easy win. We already know what to do."

They nodded in agreement. "Less small talk, more prepping boys," Fenty smiled as she walked towards them, holding a plate of food. Setting the plate down, she plopped down in her seat. "So, I'll be captain and y'all can be the crew," she giggled, spinning in the chair.

"Yeah, whatever. We all the captain. How about that?" Ben laughed.

"Okay everyone, settle down, please." The crew's heads snapped up towards the projector screen. An older woman stood on the stage awaiting the attention of the audience. She pushed her glasses back on the bridge of her nose, "Greetings everyone! I hope y'all are ready for our first annual Hack-For-Good. Today, you all will devise a plan amongst your team to defend yourselves from other groups. The timer will be here as a guide. There will be a five-minute presentation at the end from each team. The judges will make their decisions then. Good luck lads!" Applause and cheering erupted as the woman exited the stage. A loud buzz signaled to everyone that the competition had started.

Fenty began barking orders at the boys as attacks rolled in. Paper flew out of the printer beside Ben. Determined taps from keyboards and muffled conversations filled the air. Electricity ran through the atmosphere. The students were lost in the monitors, trying to successfully block and dispose of threats. "What do we do?" could be heard from a nearby section, causing Ben to chuckle in amusement. He sat back in his chair, looking at how smoothly his team was handling the incoming challenges and was proud. He had never met anyone as intelligent as them and was just happy to be working on their team. Undergraduates from the local university volunteered their time as judges. They walked around slowly inspecting each team's technique; observing their teamwork, taking notes on their communication, and problem-solving skills.

An hour and some change had gone by. The judges were now hearing the presentation of the other teams who had thrown in the towel. There were still a few attacks, however.

"I think these remaining attacks are coming from a computer somewhere. What if we hack that to stop them all? Is that the final challenge?" Ben suggested to the crew.

They all sat in silence, mulling it over. Neyo spun around in his chair and began typing into his computer. He pulled up a black terminal screen with bright green characters moving across the display. "I traced the last attack from a server. The IP address tells me it's close. Fenty, do you happen to remember some compiler language? I think if we can shut down the server by telling the computer to shut off, with an error message with our names on it, we can win this thing."

Neyo slid from the computer so Fenty could get to work. Benjamin stood up behind her, learning from the master. Within seconds, the judges were at their booth.

"How'd you hack my system?" One of the college students questioned as he sat his laptop on their table. "City Crew aka Team #3," were in blocky text across his screen. "It's nearly impossible for you guys to know how to penetrate a virtual box."

Fenty leaned back in her chair as she looked around at her associates. They all wore smug expressions. She shrugged her shoulders. "Yeah, well, this is a hackathon, right?"

Impressed, he tapped the table twice. "Y'all hang tight right here." The young man walked over to whisper to the older woman from earlier. The crew made eye contact with them.

"Looks like we got this in the bag, y'all!" Fenty squealed, getting excited. Benjamin let out a sigh of relief.

The woman took her place on stage again to gather the audience's attention. "Well, ladies and gentlemen, it seems that the hackathon has been hacked! I would like to personally congratulate and announce that Team Three has successfully defended against all threats. I would like to thank each person for helping and participating in this event. Will all the teams come to the front for pictures?"

Their bones were riddled with joy as they held up their oversized tickets to Disney World. They hugged and laughed, enjoying the feeling of success. They felt like carefree kids and could only imagine the feeling intensifying at Disney. Images of running around in the Florida sun, eating junk food and riding all the attractions danced around their thoughts.

"On three, say we did it for this picture," Fenty ordered as they threw their arms around each other. Momentary smiles were captured to be sealed away in digital memory.

Wednesday

"Mrs. Jones?" A woman's voice halted the lesson in Ben's second block class. The students were working on book assignments. Their writing utensils relieved from their duties as their ears perked at the sound of a distraction.

"Yes?" Mrs. Jones answered, not looking up from her laptop, used to the intrusion of solitude.

"May you please write a slip to send Benjamin Smith to the main office with all of his belongings?"

And with that, she clicked off. All eyes were on Ben as he sat in his seat, wondering. His palms became moist and he felt seasick as his torso lightly swayed behind the desk. Without a word, she wrote the note and held it in the air. Ben stood to his feet, feeling as if his knees would give out. *Just act cool. It's probably nothing.* But deep down, his gut felt otherwise. He focused his attention on the taps on the tile floor from his shoes instead of the whispers from the students. They were all speculating, but Benjamin knew. When he reached the office, the secretary pointed towards the conference room once he gave her his slip. Through the frosted glass, he could see familiar faces. He released a deep exhale as he pulled the door open to enter the room.

"Hey Ma," he greeted his mother as he sat down next to her in the black office chairs. Leaning back, he intertwined his fingers. "Hello Principal Holts and Coach Freeman."

They both nodded back at him. Benjamin could feel the heat coming off of his mother. "Benjamin, do you know why I have called you here today?" Principal Holts questioned.

Ben's bottom lip folded into his mouth as he stared at Coach Freeman. They had not broken eye contact since he sat down. Finally, Ben glanced down to fully take in the moment. He knew what was about to happen. There was no reason to even fight it. He felt defeated because he was defeated.

"Yes, Principal Holts, I do know why I am here. I am here because the educational system you are 'providing' is laughable. This is a glorified daycare. The teachers YOU hired are clearly not trained to handle situations in a reasonable manner. If I was an authoritative figure and I saw someone leaving, maybe I'd question myself and then them. I-"

"That is enough!" His mother exploded. "Where did all this lip come from Benjamin? Your father and I did not raise you to speak like this!"

"Well, you and father aren't really raising me anymore," he countered. Without hesitation, Kimberly backhanded Benjamin in his lip.

"Now whoa! Wait a minute there, Mrs. Smith!" Coach Freeman yelled, jumping up before the situation could escalate any further.

"How dare you talk to me that way after all I have sacrificed for this family? For you?" She gasped, pointing her index finger at him. Benjamin, I just-" she stopped to shake her head in disbelief. The emotions from the commotion was too much. She was feeling like the walls were moving closer into her personal space.

"Mrs. Smith, I'll make this quick. Unfortunately, we have to expel Benjamin from this school," Principal Holts said apologetically. He was looking into the eyes of a broken woman.

"Expel?" Kimberly and Benjamin repeated in unison.

"Isn't that a little too much? We're just going to skip over suspension? Detention? All of that?" Her anger was now being redirected toward the new source of bad news.

"Benjamin was warned beforehand about his behavior and explicitly ignored the administered punishment."

Kimberly glanced over at Benjamin again. He sat with tightly balled fists and lips. Furrowed brows displaying his dissatisfaction with the entire spectacle. *This can't be my life right now.* He let out a slight chuckle as he shook his head.

Principal Holts shot a stern look at Benjamin. "You will also be disqualified from attending the trip to Disney World with your teammates."

"Disney World?" Kimberly questioned again. This was new information to her.

"Benjamin entered a hackathon held within the school and won. He needed a parent's signature to participate," he informed her.

Crap.

"Wow Benjamin," Kimberly said in sarcastic disbelief, her tone deep. "So, you're just out here skipping school? Running the streets? Forging signatures? Huh?!" she yelled, letting her emotions get the best of her. Her voice had risen a few pitches. "That's what you're doing? That's what you're choosing to do? What happened to my little boy, huh?" Her voice cracked as her hand flew to her mouth. "No, I am not going to keep crying over Smith men anymore. You want to be a man Benjamin, then you go be one because I obviously can't raise a man." She stood up to leave. "Principal Holts, is there anything else to discuss and handle here? I need to make a phone call."

Principal Holts slid the expulsion papers in front of her. She quickly signed them and walked out of the office. Benjamin sat silently, nodding his head, digesting the drama that just unfolded.

"Principal Holts, Fenty and Neyo do get to go, right?"

"Yes."

Ben nodded again and clapped his hands together before standing to his feet. "It's been nice, gentlemen." He said before also exiting the room. Ben left that office, knowing his life was about to change forever. He was transitioning into a man.

The car ride home was quiet. Besides his mom's side-eyes and random grumblings, there was no interaction between them. Kimberly was under the impression that her son had morphed into this horrendous bad boy. That this new disobedient attitude had to be the result of her bad parenting.

"Benjamin, " Kimberly said, pulling into the driveway of their home. "I love you. But I can't do this. I can't do your father's part. I can't raise a man." She took a deep breath. "Therefore, I've decided to send you to Montana to stay with your Uncle James for a while. You can visit me and your dad on breaks and holidays, but you need discipline that I can't give." She studied Ben's face for a reaction, but received none. He continued to look straight ahead.

"Okay, Ma. Whatever you say," he said, getting out of the car and heading towards his room. *Yup, I guess this is my life.*

Chapter 6: Slippery Slope

Days had passed by as Benjamin laid in his bed, feeling every emotion known to the spectrum. His mom basically didn't want him anymore. His father was wherever doing whatever with whoever. He was losing his friends. Life had changed so drastically. His mother came to his doorway to try to talk a few times, but Ben kept his face blank and found that eventually, she'd retreat. Kimberly thought it would be best to work from home for a few days until Benjamin's father came back into town. She set up her workstation at the breakfast nook. Every so often, Ben would trudge downstairs wrapped in his black comforter, grab a few apple slices, cheese bites and a bottle of water. He did not come down for dinner or verbally respond to her. He was just there. She began second guessing her decision, but decided she had to do whatever it took to make sure her son would stay out of trouble. The last thing she wanted to do was ignore him and push him into harm's way. *Sending him to be with James for a few is the right idea.* She had to constantly reassure herself.

Looking down at her laptop and the scattered papers around it, she ran her hand through her hair. She sighed again, before resting her forehead against the tabletop.

"Mom, can I at least go tell my friends what happened? You took my laptop and phone," Ben pleaded with his mom. She looked up to see him standing on the last stair, dressed in his basketball gear.

"Yeah. Here," she handed him his phone from her purse. "You better call me when you get to them. And don't be gone too long." He just nodded before walking out of the house.

Ben hopped on his bike, heading toward Fenty and Neyo's apartment. Arriving in minutes, he tossed the bike to the side of their door and waited for an answer.

"Well, well, well, look who finally popped up," Neyo greeted as he moved to the side to let Ben in. Fenty was sitting with her legs crossed on the sofa. She glanced up at him and rolled her eyes.

"Now I know you're not going to treat me like that?" Ben asked, coming to sit beside her. Neyo plopped down in the loveseat across from them.

"You know we heard what happened?" Neyo informed.

"Yeah, I'm sure."

"So, couldn't you have come to us then?" Fenty asked with her arms crossed, resting on her chest.

Ben held his head down as he played with his fingers. "Yeah, I should have, but I didn't want you guys thinking we couldn't enter. I still wanted y'all to be able to go," he explained. "Looking back, yeah, I guess I should have said something. I just didn't want to upset y'all, especially if he wasn't even serious."

"What Coach did was stupid. He sees the football players leave all the time. Why hate on our shine?" Neyo interjected.

"My thoughts exactly, but we're still 'kids' so obviously nothing we say matters." Ben just shook his head. "Well, either way, I asked Principal Holts if y'all would still be going, and he was like "yeah". So y'all just have enough fun for me too." Ben sunk back in his seat, thinking about the fun he could have had with his friends.

"We're going regardless," Fenty chuckled. "What you

had going on had nothing to do with us. You're family, but sometimes, we all have to handle uncomfortable stuff on our own."

"Speaking of 'on my own'," Ben paused. "Well, my mom thinks it's a good idea to send me away."

"For the summer?"

"Forever, I guess," Ben shrugged his shoulders, not having a concrete answer. He was unsure of how long this move would last.

"Wow, so what did your dad say? Or have you spoken to him?" Fenty asked, straightening her back.

"I haven't talked to him. My mom took my phone and stuff."

"He hasn't called you on her phone?" Ben was silent. "Well, whatevah. How much longer do we have with you?" Fenty asked, trying to lighten the mood.

"According to her, I leave in a few days. I'll have to pack my stuff up so they can ship them to Montana. "

"Montana?" Neyo's lip curled in confusion.

"My uncle works for the government and he stays out that way. Honestly, I don't understand how she thought this was a good idea, but whatever. It's not like I have any real control," Ben's tone was low and somber. His feelings were still hurt over the situation. Everything just felt unfair to him. He had lived the majority of his life following his parents' orders. He was obedient. He listened. He wasn't much of a rebel. But now that he wanted to take control of his life, things seemed to turn upside down. Questioning thoughts rested at the base of his throat like hot coal.

"Well, let's not think about it until the time comes," Fenty bumped his shoulder. "You need help packing?"

Ben looked up in contemplation. "That's actually not a

bad idea. I do need the help. Let me ask my warden if it'd be okay." They all chuckled at his joke. For the rest of the time, they caught up on chit chat about different shows they watched together, new music that was released, posts from social media and just chilling. Benjamin felt like himself around them. He had a voice and he felt like it mattered to them. The sun started to set when he realized he'd have to return to his cell soon. He said his goodbyes with hopes of visiting his friends tomorrow.

Ben tossed his bike on the side of the house as he entered his home. He had beat the sun home from pedaling like lightning. His mom's car was still in the driveway and the kitchen light was on. She was sitting at the table, working on her laptop. Their eyes connected once he stood in the doorway.

"Hey Ma," he greeted, hanging his jacket up on the coat rack.

She gave him a tight smile. "Had fun?"

"Yeah. We just hung out. I was wondering if they could come over to help me pack. Then you'd finally get to meet them." He grabbed a water from the fridge. Leaning against the side of it, he stopped to give her his attention.

"Mmm, will their parents be dropping them off?"

"Fenty's mom is a nurse and Neyo stays with them. We can give you her number though, so you can call. I know how you like to check out everything."

"Sarcasm?" Her left eyebrow shot up with a smirk resting on her face. "You still got jokes ?"

Ben playfully rolled his eyes. "Yeah, I'm just letting you know, Ma." He gave her a light smile. It felt good to smile at her.

"Okay. I don't mind. I'll let you know when you should

start packing up. I'll be doing a half day at the office tomorrow, so I'll be back in the afternoon. Did you have plans to be over there all summer?"

"I mean, it gets kinda lonely here," he responded, while stuffing his hands in his pockets.

"Well, I'd appreciate it if you spent some time here when you're not so busy. We could catch a movie or something. I still like you, you know." Kimberly slightly closed her laptop. Benjamin tightened his lips. *That's not what I've been feeling.*

She noticed his expression. "So, no time?"

He shrugged his shoulders. "I guess we can, Ma," he said, before making his way towards the stairs. "I'm going to go and get ready for bed." he jogged up the stairs, leaving Kimberly to watch his back.

Benjamin sat in his bed, staring at the ceiling. He could hear the hums and squeaks of the house settling while they rest from outside his door. His body was relaxed as he snuggled deep into his cover cocoon. His eyes focused on the spinning of the ceiling fan until his eyelids slowly closed.

"Benjamin! Please come in and sit down! It's so great to finally meet you," a voice boomed over him in excitement. The knuckles of both his index fingers rubbed his eyes vigorously. His vision felt weird. The place where his eyes should have been felt hollow. Accepting the sensation and more curious about his surroundings, Ben stuck his arms out in front of him. Everything seemed dark and spotty. He felt like he was opening his eyes underwater when he focused on a table in the distance. Stumbling, he grabbed the back of the chair once he reached the table. There was loud rock music blasting from a speaker that felt directly over him. The melody made his skin crawl.

"Hello?" he called out, sitting in the seat and fingers intertwined in his lap. His breathing was slow as oxygen traveled past his lips. There was no response. He felt as though pressure was being applied to his throat.

"Benjamin, Hi." As if on cue, his vision became clear and a spotlight hung above the black metal surface. Ben squinted as he tried to make out a face from the figure sitting in front of him. It wore a black hoodie with their arms folded on top of the table. "You've been very impactful in my projects. I thought it was time we finally met."

"C. Murphy?"

"That's my username. But yes, that's me."

"Who are you?" Ben's eyebrows furrowed as his temper started to flair. "Where am I? What's going on here?"

"You ask a lot more questions in person. I didn't think you were like this," he replied coolly, leaning back in his seat. The darkness surrounding them continued to hide his identity.

"Okay, so you met me, now what?" he spat in a low tone. He wasn't being too fond of being kidnapped. "Where am I?"

"You're at home, Benjamin. But we need to talk." Murphy's hands came back into the light but were still pitch black. Ben's eyes widened. The place where nails would have been bright red and a healthy amount of black dirt underneath. "See Benny Boy, this darkness here is my home. I have to navigate the shadows so people like you can live for me. I know what's going on in your home."

"What's going on?" His heart raced. *Am I dreaming?*

"Your parents' divorce. It's so sad. Shouldn't have happened. But it did. And I know you're angry. Sooo angry. But I also know you haven't been getting that anger out. It's okay to be angry. Use that anger to make you better. Let your anger make others angry. That's how you feel better. Give your anger away. Let me help you give your anger away."

Ben remained silent. He was confused from all the emotions flowing through him at the moment. Whatever this Murphy man was saying was insane, but he was curious. Something clawed from the achy part in his heart to know more. He wanted an outlet to release the pain that his parents had recklessly dumped on him. Because it was true. He was mad. He had been collecting shards of anger over the last several months. "How can I get rid of it?"

A bright light appeared from the hoodie. Only white teeth were displayed. "Let me help you, help me. Find me a weak spot in this system and watch the world feel your pain." He slid a gold shipping envelope across the table.

"That's all I have to do?"

"Yup, that's all."

"What's in it for me?" Ben shot back.

"Smart boy. Well, what do you want?"

Ben went silent. He had no idea what he really wanted, besides wanting to rid his body of the pain he couldn't control. This was a dream anyways so why not shoot high. "I need fifteen thousand dollars deposited into my account immediately."

"Done," he slid a laptop from the darkness. "Find it."

Ben swallowed and began nibbling at the right corner of his mouth. *Air Lines Pilot Association?* He inspected the system, and then extracted their code. He remembered techniques that he had learned from the crew on how to hack certain unknown sites carefully. Quickly, he tapped away at the keys as his brain raced with answers. He was in overdrive as his mind had laser like aim on his target. He built firewalls to protect his identity and traced cookies for history logs. He soon discovered a decrypted password from a recent login, copied it and created a spoof account. He slid the laptop back around. "You now have an unknown account that won't show on their registry list in the database, but you will go unsuspected because you're using a duplicated key."

"I knew you were the man to talk to."

"Ahhh!" Ben screamed, sitting up in his bed. Sweat drenched his body as he observed his environment. He was back at home. *Was I having a bad dream?* His breathing was rapid until he was able to calm himself. He snatched his phone from his desk and checked his currency account. Three thousand dollars had been deposited. His eyes widened again. *What is going on?* He sat at the edge of his bed, trying to figure everything out. *What did I do?*

Some days had passed and Ben reasoned with himself that he just got a bonus from C. Murphy and the dream was just weird. He chalked it up to a nightmare and pushed the thoughts out of his mind. *Just enjoy the moment,* he thought as he walked briskly behind Fenty with Neyo closely behind him. He looked back at Neyo. "Do you know who she's on the phone with?" Fenty called him and demanded he get on his bike to meet them at the train station. Code red. So Benjamin leapt into action and beat them there. Now they were rushing to catch the evening train downtown with no explanation. Neyo shrugged his shoulders with a goofy expression, causing Ben to fold in laughter. They were always up for Fenty's random adventures around the city. She was the ringleader to their pact.

"Uh Fenty, where are we going? Neyo dumb butt doesn't know either," he said, tapping her shoulder once they were standing on the train.

Fenty scoffed at both his question and the guy that bumped into her, shuffling down the aisle. "Our cousin, Megan, is in town so, we're going to meet her. It's been years since I saw her back on the island."

Neyo repeated his previous gesture, causing them all laugh. "You don't ever know nothing," Ben laughed. "But that's cool, though. How'd she make it all the way here?"

"She's in college, so I guess it has something to do with it. I don't really know, but she messaged me online saying 'meet up' so here we are." Ben nodded as he looked out at the scenery transition from tunnels to streets as they sped through the town. Within minutes, they were at Midtown station following Fenty's GPS to a clothing boutique.

"Cousin has money if she's down here shopping like this," Neyo commented as he noticed the luxury cars and upscale buildings. Even the sidewalks were clean. Silky dogs' collars matched their owners in some kind of way. They were a long way from their neighborhood.

When they entered the store, a brown skinned woman that favored Fenty ran up to them. Long braids hung down her back. "Hey Titi," she greeted, embracing Fenty. Fenty returned the excitement and hugged her family. "It's been forever. You're a grown woman now," she teased, poking Fenty in her cheeks.

"Oh girl, bye!" they giggled together. "You remember Neyo. If not, it's cool. He ain't important," she introduced, still giggling.

"I remember you too, lil' cuz. Come on over here," she pulled him into a tight hug.

"This is our new adopted cousin, Benjamin," Fenty pointed. She grabbed him for a hug too. "Ben, this is our big cousin, Megan. As you can see, she's awesome." Admiration twinkled in Fenty's eyes. Benjamin and Neyo just watched their interaction.

"I'm flattered, little one. You're quite poppin' yourself," she counter complimented. "Hey, so I need to find some outfits for a conference I have coming up, where's a good mall?" Fenty grabbed her hand and guided her out of the store. Megan began laughing. "That's not the spot, huh?"

"No, girl. Are you driving or what?"

"Well,. I was trying to learn the metro system down here since I'll be here for a while."

"What's a while?"

"Oh, just the summer," she said smiling. Fenty squealed in excitement.

"Oh my gawsh! Tis' is going to be like old times," Fenty's accent untamed from the news. "I'm sorry, I'm letting you know now that I'm always going to be with you."

"That's fine. You know I don't mind. So, come on, where is this mall?"

Fenty smiled at her big cousin. They were five years apart, but as close as sisters. Once Fenty had to move to the States, it got hard to see each other. But now they were older, their bond could be reignited. The ride to Lenox Mall up north was filled with memories from their homeland. Funny stories and photos of their life journey were exchanged. Ben enjoyed learning more about his friends' personalities and their past. They rarely talked about their family life, so this was interesting. Megan demanded the route through the mall start at the food court and offered to buy everyone lunch. Of course,. the hungry teens took a free meal of their choosing.

"So, Ben, what's your story? You've been awfully quiet," Megan commented while stuffing bourbon chicken and rice into her mouth.

"He hasn't been able to, with you and Fen looking all over the place," Neyo teased.

"Well , maybe I shouldn't have fed you," she twirled her fork at him, smirking.

"My story is simple. I grew up here. I go to school with your cousins. We met in a techy chat online. Now we're all here."

Megan nodded. "Simple cookie. Okay."

"Ben, Megan is getting a degree in psychology. She'd be a good person to talk to," Fenty gently offered, knowing his situation. "She helps me out a lot when I go through stuff."

Ben just nodded, feeling shy. He didn't want to withdraw, but he felt bad remembering everything that transpired.

"It's cool. Ben can talk when he's ready. Just know that pain doesn't last forever. And you're never alone," she said, patting his shoulder before standing to throw away her empty food container.

"Dang cuz, you vacuumed that food down," Neyo injected. laughing.

"Boy, whatever," she said, rolling her eyes. "I'm ready to shop. Let's go" Megan directed, walking towards the elevator. The rest followed suit and headed towards the shops with her. However, Benjamin kept repeating what she said in his mind. *Pain doesn't last forever.*

Chapter 7: Plane Crash

"So, your mom hasn't mentioned anything about you having to move, has she?" Fenty questioned as they laid in the grass in the quad. The three amigos were waiting on Megan to get out of a class she was taking at a local HBCU downtown. It was a nice, hot day in the city. It was towards the end of July and the humidity could choke a horse if it wasn't in the shade.

"Nope. Not even a bit. Actually, she's just been gone a lot like before, so we don't really have time to talk. We text every day though."

"What about your dad?"

"Yeah, he texted me earlier today, asking if I was going to get on the game later. He's like a distant homeboy now," Ben reflected on his relationship with the people that birthed him. They were doing their own thing while he enjoyed a free summer. Every year, his mom made him go to summer camp, but this year since she couldn't afford it, as long as he promised to not get into trouble again, she was cool. Kimberly believed that maybe some trust in their relationship would be a good thing.

"Hey, why is Meg down here anyways? I thought she went to school up north?" Neyo interjected, thinking aloud.

"She does, but she wants extra credits to graduate early. She's thinking about moving here or Texas." They'd been spending a lot of time with Megan. She introduced them to new settings and ways of life. They felt fancy with her and not like little kids. They had been spent the last few weeks linking with Megan when she was free and working for C.

Murphy online when they had time. They had saved up during the school year, so they weren't in dire need of money. The summer had been filled with visiting new attractions around the city, a couple of festivals and concerts that were at Piedmont Park and hanging out at new restaurants.

"Hello lovebugs," Megan sang, popping her head over them. They squinted for a second, taking in her image before sitting up. She tossed her folder in the grass between them and sat down. "How would y'all like to go with me to Myrtle Beach for the weekend? I don't have class this Friday and my god mom has a condo out there." She shrugged her shoulders. "It sounds fun just to get away and reset."

"Especially before school starts back," Fenty added with Ben and Neyo adding in. The last week of August meant they were moving up in the academic food chain.

"Before you know it, y'all will be graduating. My babies," she fakes crying, pulling them all into a hug.

"Well, we have to get permission first. We're not that grown like you yet," Neyo stated for the crew. They still wanted to be respectful of their parents' rules.

"Yeah, of course, duh," she rolled her eyes, laughing. "I'm not getting charged for kidnapping. Just let me know in the group message. We can leave early in the morning and get there in the afternoon. Then come back Sunday afternoon. Sounds like a plan?"

They all agreed and lingered on the quad for a little while longer. Megan was always telling them crazy stories about her professors, the students she had to work with on projects, random people in the offices. They were entertaining and kept Ben's mind off of his own issues. The whole summer, he was on edge about if his mom was really going to make him move. He didn't want to bring it up, but he wanted to know. He had finally come out of his shell and made real friends. And to snatch all that away seemed cruel. *Hopefully, she'll just forget about all of it.* He had been plotting on proposing that they all move to a new school. They could ride the metro to get there and it'd be a better quality of education. That way, they could be challenged instead of bored out their minds. But he kept his hope to himself in fear that his mom's decision would ruin all of that.

After getting food, they all separated to head home. Benjamin was surprised to see his mother at home in their living room. The TV mirrored her computer screen. A lamp and several candles provided enough light for a calm mood. Kimberly looked up to see her son standing in the doorway with questioning eyes. She too was still pondering on her decision. She couldn't turn back on it. He would know her threats meant nothing. But how could she possibly follow through and let her only child go? Daily, she paced back and forth in her mind, causing her to avoid her son. His whole future was in her shaky hands and yet she didn't even know how to see her own. *A lot of pressure for one woman.* He took a sip of lemon water.

"Hey Benny," she greeted him with a smile. He returned her gesture with a small one of his own. She hoped that she hid the uneasiness within her from her son. She was a hot mess on the inside, but had her face ironed for the world. "How's it going?"

He shrugged his shoulder. "Pretty good. So, you remember me telling you about my friend's cousin, Megan?" She nodded. "Well, she asked if it would be okay for us to go with her to Myrtle Beach for the weekend. You can have her number and meet her, please just let me go. I've been on my best behavior all summer, Ma," he began, pleading his case.

Kimberly's eyebrows shot up at his excitement. "Why are you so hype about this?"

"Cause, I just want to hang out with my friends. I don't know how much longer I'm going to be able to do that," Ben answered honestly, stuffing his hands in his pockets.

Kim's bottom lip pushed upwards in response to his comment, her head slightly tilting. *Okay.* "Yeah, I don't mind. Enjoy yourself." Ben thanked her and told her all the important details. She had access to Ben's real-time GPS location via his smartphone, so she was not too worried. However, his comment bothered her. *Is that how he really feels?* Ben headed upstairs, elated and planning his outfits for the trip.

"Alright, everybody got their snacks, blankets and electronics for this trip?" Megan announced as she pulled her car away from Benjamin's house. It was six in the morning. She had just picked up the crew and talked to everyone's parents. The road trip would be roughly six hours, plus rest stops and gas refills. They all had playlists set for the drive. There were chargers available in case devices started dying. Megan talked to them about the rules of the road, how to travel safely and ideas about activities to do. Eventually, the ride was over and they arrived at a high rise building around two o'clock. Glass covered the building completely.

"Whooaaa," the teens sang in unison as they entered the condo through the kitchen. Stainless steel appliances filled the room. The fully furnished home was nicely decorated and smelled of fresh scents. Tile and bleached wood floors ran throughout the suite. Each person was able to have their own bed. A balcony was attached to the suite that overlooked the beach. The waves crashing on the shore provided a soothing soundtrack.

"So y'all like it?" Megan asked, plopping down on the sofa.

"We love it!" they exclaimed before bursting into laughter.

"Perfect. So, we can rest for a minute and go out to explore the town," she informed. She got up to lay in her desired bedroom for the trip while the others remained on the balcony, taking in the view. About an hour later, they were leaving in search of food and fun. They found themselves at an Escape Room where they'd have to solve different puzzles to defuse an imaginary bomb in a certain amount of time. Once they left there, they got some ice cream and walked along the beach at night until they were ready to turn in.

Saturday was all about fun in the sun. Megan planned the day from the time they woke up until it was time to sleep. Waking up and getting ready for the day began around 10 a.m. Visiting local museums, shops and attractions on the boardwalk was scheduled for the afternoon until around five o'clock. They returned to the condo to get cleaned up for dinner, which was at eight o'clock. Ben suggested walking their meal off on the shore before calling it a night. Neyo and Fenty walked ahead, playfully pushing and shoving each other.

"Benjamin, you know what I noticed about you," Megan said out of nowhere. They were casually strolling along.

The sand and cold water rushing over their feet gave them pleasant goosebumps. He made eye contact with her and raised his eyebrows. "You get angry and instead of expressing that, you just shut down."

He was silent for a moment as he thought about her comment. "What made you bring this up?"

"Well, I noticed earlier that you got a text from your mom. Your nose flared, but you never said anything. Honestly, it's impressive because I wouldn't be able to do that," she chuckled. "I know grown people that wouldn't be able to do that. But it's not healthy."

"How is it not?" He glanced at her, giving his full attention. Maybe she knew how to get rid of the confusion and pain he was hiding deep down.

"Because you're not fully expressing yourself, so everything is just bottled up. And you know what happens when you keep shaking a bottled soda? It explodes. And I just don't want to explode in the wrong setting or with the wrong person. Trust me, I know from experience."

Ben nodded as he digested her words. "So, what should I do? I don't know how to say everything I feel sometimes. It's just like I don't have the words to describe the feelings."

"It sounds like you need some therapy."

"I'm not crazy," Ben retorted defensively.

"I never said you were. But everyone needs someone to talk to that knows how to talk back to them. Therapists and counselors are people trained for years on how gently handling the human mind. I've been to therapy more times than I can count," she admitted.

"You? For what? Your life seems perfect."

"Me? Very far from it, baby boy. But counseling helped

me get through a lot, even now. There are free hotlines that you can call or text just to vent. They won't judge you or tell your parents or anything like that. It's a safe place."

Ben nodded in understanding. "I guess it wouldn't hurt to look into it since you recommended it."

"Yeah, it helps a lot. You didn't hear this from me, but I know Fenty and Neyo have started using the hotline to get comfortable with counseling too." Ben's face made an astonished expression, causing Meg to giggle. "Yeah, see? Everyone needs a little help sometimes."

Ben remained silent and just let the beat of the waves guide them back to their suite. He appreciated the conversation shared with Megan. She had become like a big sister to all of them. Whenever they needed help, advice or a place to run away to, she was there for them. He looked out into the darkness and felt a surge of emotions. Kimberly texted him earlier, confirming that he would be moving to Montana for the school year and to be ready to start packing upon his return. He stopped to allow a few feet of distance between himself and the others. He stood there, studying the stars' shimmer on top of the black water. The moon's bright reflection illuminating the sky. *I can live every day by the sea.* He felt at peace. Untouchable. For a few moments on the beach, he felt hopeful with life. Clearly, nobody was perfect and that was okay. It was okay to not be okay.

Sunday morning, they awoke to catch breakfast at a restaurant within walking distance from their building. When they returned, they decided to rest for an hour before getting back on the road. Benjamin decided to break the news to the crew on Monday. For now, he was enjoying his company with his best friends.

"Benjamin, your uncle is here!" Kimberly hollered up the stairs.

Her brother, James, greeted her with a warm side hug. "How are you holding up, sis?"

She let out a long sigh. "I'm holding," she was silent for a second as she mulled over her decision one last time. "You really think this is a good idea for him?" Her nerves were wrecked and she had been up all night in contemplation.

"Look, he's in safe hands. You need a break to get yourself together and he needs a male figure to guide him. I don't mind stepping in until things are smoothed out. You know I got your back, Kim."

She bit her bottom lip as she nodded. Yes, in theory, everything sounded reasonable, but she was still unsure. "I just don't want him to hate me, you know?"

"He won't hate you. When he gets older, he'll understand. For right now, just don't worry about it. You're doing the best that you can." He hugged her again before jogging up the stairs towards Ben's room. His friends sat on his bed while he was zipping up his last suitcase. "Hi, I'm called Uncle James around these parts," he said, introducing himself to the teens. They gave shy waves back and excused themselves downstairs.

"So, do I get my own room or what because this was never discussed with me. I don't want to be sleeping in your shoe closet, Unc," Ben joked. He didn't mind going to spend time with his favorite relative, it was leaving behind his best friends that was the problem.

"You'll see when you get there, kiddo. You almost ready?"

86

Benjamin took a look around the room he grew up in. Posters from his favorite sports teams, music artists that he liked and some pictures of him as a baby, adorned the walls. He had packed a good amount of his belongings, but decided to leave some for when he came back to visit. "Yeah, just give me a second. Has my dad come yet?"

"Nah, not yet. But your mom said he was on the way. Just a lot of traffic," he responded, rubbing the back of his neck.

Ben just nodded. He believed his dad when he said he'd visit to send him off properly, but Darnell had been acting flakey lately. Game times they had arranged, he'd been missing. Texts were getting harder to get a response. Phone calls were directed to voicemail. *I guess he had something better to do.* With one last look, he glanced around the room, grabbed his luggage and headed downstairs. Everyone migrated from the living room to outside to help Ben load up the rental car. They stood around having small talk as a car pulled in front of the driveway. His dad hopped out, carrying a blue gift bag.

"I was on the way, but then, I was like 'my son needs to be fresh'. So, I stopped to grab you a few things," he said, handing him the bag as he approached the small crowd. "I remember you two." He pointed at Fenty and Neyo. Again, they gave a friendly wave as they slid on both sides of Ben.

Peeking into his bag, they saw Nike clothing articles and a card. "Thanks, Dad. I appreciate it." They gave a warm embrace. Ben wanted to be upset, but having his father present dissolved some of the feelings. He stuffed the clothes into his carry-on duffle bag. "Well, I guess this is it," he said, looking around at his family. Fenty had puppy eyes and Neyo's hands were stuffed into his pockets.

Kimberly had tears in the base of her eyes as she tried to keep her emotions at bay. *He comes with guilt gifts while I have to send our son away.* She gave Darnell a long hard stare before he felt her watching him. Uneasy, he shifted his weight from one foot to another.

"Megan said she's sorry she couldn't come, but sends her love," Fenty whispered into his ear as she gave him a tight embrace. Neyo joined in as the adults watched.

"I'm sure you'll make new friends, but just remember, they're not going to treat you as well as us," Neyo joked, offering his infamous side grin. Ben just nudged him with his shoulder.

"I love you, Benny. I'm so sorry all this had to happen this way," his mom apologized, hugging him.

It didn't have to be, he thought.

"Let's get going. The flight is in a few hours. You know how traffic and airport security can get," Uncle James reminded. Ben nodded and said his farewells one last time before climbing into the vehicle. Looking out the front passenger window, Ben watched his parents trail after the car. In the rear-view mirror, he saw Fenty and Neyo ride away on their bikes back towards their home.

"Hey, everything seems kinda funky right now, but it'll get better. Trust me," Uncle James said, trying to offer Ben some reassurance. He just nodded like always and sat back, ready for the next chapter in his life.

A few hours later

"Flight 1123AKJ to Central Tower. We are having some navigation issues. The aircraft seems to keep nose-diving," the pilot of the plane informed the command station. "I need an override to the system." Radio silence. The pilot glanced over at his co-pilot. "Flight 1123AKJ to Central Tower, I repeat, I need access to a system override."

Loud white noise blasted through the headphones, causing Pilot Chaplin to wince in pain. Simultaneously, the plane began nose diving again. Pilot Chaplin yanked at the steering wheel in an attempt to level the plane. Co-pilot, Legan, scrambled to find a button that would disable the automatic flying system. Behind the doors, sounds of horrific shrills filled the cabin. Banging from the flight attendants caused Legan to jump. He glanced at Chaplin and then watched the Earth become closer.

"It was an honor flying with you sir," Legan said, leaning back in his seat. There was nothing that could be done. The plane was flying them straight to hell based on its own computer system. Chaplin let go, and shook hands with his friend of twelve years. Chaos was erupting behind the door. There was nothing they could say to the passengers. A "sorry" was not going to suffice for their lives or calm their nerves. They were all headed to their final destination.

"Um, Benjamin, please call me as soon as you land. Please. I just need to make sure you're okay," Kimberly cried into the phone. Darnell sat beside her with his eyes glued to the television screen. Multiple news outlets were announcing the fatal crash for a plane leaving the south towards Montana. The authorities were unsure of any survivors and no other information had been revealed to the public. Kimberly and Darnell sat there terrified. Kimberly had lost all of her marbles as she panicked about losing her only son and brother.

Darnell was doing his best to be a support system.

"There are plenty of flights, Kim. I'm sure he's okay. Just keep the faith. He'll give us a call as soon as he lands." *Please let him call as soon as he lands,* they both thought as they sat in silence, awaiting any changes in the news.

Chapter 8: Hello Montana

"Um, Benjamin please call me-" He removed the phone from his ear to check the time. *Why is she tripping? She just saw me.* Shaking his head, he looked at his phone quizzically and put it away in his pocket. He was trying to stay caught up with Uncle James as they exited the plane and into the main terminal. As they passed by, he could see some passengers crying and consoling each other. "Hey Unc, you have any idea about what's going on?" Ben's chin abruptly collided with his uncle's back.

"The flight scheduled an hour before ours crashed," he informed, looking up from his phone. He too was receiving mass calls and texts pertaining to his safety. "Let me make a few calls real quick. I think you should call your mom back," James said, before stepping a few steps off to the side.

"Hey Ma," Ben greeted his mother. The call was one-sided, with Ben answering a few questions here and there. She was frightened by the coincidence and honestly, Ben was a little suspicious too. James walked back over, signaling that it was time to make a move. Ben said his goodbyes and they were off towards the parking garage. Music from a local radio station filled the car ride to his new home. He assumed the road home would be winding mountain trails, huge towering trees and larger-than-life deer skipping in front of cars. Instead, it looked like a regular city, with regular people. Until Uncle James made a sharp left into some woods off the main road from town. The luxury off-road car was made for a few bumps and turns.

"So, what are you thinking? I see you looking around," James commented. Benjamin just shrugged his shoulders. "Yeah, it isn't much, but it's peaceful. I mean, look at the sky. Tell me if you've seen a sky like that in Georgia."

"I thought it was all one sky," Ben grinned, observing the blue blanket above.

"Nah. This is Big Sky Country out here. You'll see what I mean." He just nodded and continued looking out the window. They arrived at a multi-story home built with a multitude of tan rocks, the jagged edges fitting together perfectly like bricks. There was a long driveway to the house, which sat in the middle of a wooded area.

"You live here?" Ben asked. James just chuckled at his reaction. He had underestimated his uncle's worth and was shocked. James never presented himself as the flashy type. However, after hanging out with Meg all summer, he knew his uncle was important. They exited the vehicle and entered the home through the attached garage. Once inside the home, hardwood floors, high vaulted ceilings and floor-to-ceiling windows gave a modern vibe. The same rocks that adorned the outside, were inside too. "So, I definitely need a tour of your place," he said, nodding in approval. He smiled, rubbing his hands together. *Maybe this won't be so bad after all.*

"After I show you to your living quarters." They hauled Ben's belongings into the west wing of the home. "My room and office are just two doors down."

"What's on the other side of your house?"

"Storage really." Ben nodded and James could see how anxious he was to explore the home. "C'mon, let's give you your tour. You're about to break your neck from looking around so hard," James joked. James took Ben room by room and let him look around. The kitchen was built for a professional chef, with stainless steel appliances and a smart fridge. There was a home gym with an indoor sauna. Every workout equipment imaginable was there. The den housed his entire video game collection. Various consoles with hundreds of accompanying games, headphones and colored controllers were placed neatly in designated cubicles. Attached to the den was a game room with ping pong, air hockey and pool table. A corner of the room was dedicated to vintage arcade games and a VR station. He had an actual machine that moved and flipped you around in a simulation! There was a wine cellar that held infinite bottles in little holes to the ceiling. Ben picked up one dating back to 1926.

"Mmm, exquisite taste nephew," James smirked, taking the bottle from Ben's hand.

"Mom and Dad know you out here in Montana living like this?" Ben laughed in astonishment. He felt like he was strolling through one of his mom's Home Interior magazines, mountain edition.

"They visited once when I was remodeling some years ago, but I was at my apartment near downtown then," he answered. "I try to keep it private. Only a select few know where I live and I spend a lot of time here, so I need it to be my ultimate sanctuary."

"So, you won't be having any extra visitors?"

"You mean my lady friends? Nobody besides your soon-to-be aunt."

Ben's ears lit up at the mention of his uncle's long-time girlfriend. Hadn't seen her in a few years, but would hear her name when he'd eavesdrop during their conversations.

"You mean, I might get to see Miss Tiana? She always brought the best gifts," he said, smiling.

"Maybe. You know how she is now," he shrugged his shoulders. This conversation was too high brow for Ben. "You get settled in and I'll be around. We can meet up later in the game room to watch some movies or something," he said before walking off down the hall. Ben spun towards the huge mountain range on display behind him. Everything in the home just screamed fancy to him. The professional design team could pass it off as a hotel. Throughout the home were seating areas awaiting long hours with a good book. Fancy art hung at precise angles dressed the walls. There were large bay windows in some of the bathrooms that allowed one to feel like they were bathing in nature. This was the home he deserved. He just wished Fenty and Neyo could enjoy the beauty too.

After weeks of strolling around the property alone, Ben soon realized that Uncle James would be a hands-off type of guardian. He'd see him off in the mornings and they'd talk in the evenings when James returned. He didn't have to worry about cooking because a cook had stopped by to meal prep for the week. His only major responsibility was completing the online courses. The work was easy to follow so he was able to finish the first three chapters in one sitting. But he found himself bored. The work with C. Murphy didn't seem worth it anymore. It was better when he was doing it with his friends.

"Hey, you want to go to the national park tomorrow? I just have to run to the base to pick up some files then we can head out," James invited, startling Ben out of a daydream in the den.

Ben's head snapped in the direction of his uncle's voice

behind him. "Uh, you know I don't own any 'outdoors' clothes, right?" He grinned at him.

James shook his head. "Well, it looks like we'll stop by the mall too. Are you hungry? I'm about to warm up my food."

"Yeah, I'll take a plate," he said, hopping off the leather sectional. They spent the rest of the night watching old cartoons and playing some of James' favorite video games. Around midnight, James found himself talking to no one because Ben had dozed off to sleep. He woke him up and they parted ways for slumber.

"Did you remember to bring your passport?" James questioned Ben as they arrived at the gates of a military base. Armed guards paced in front of the gate, checking the identification of each passenger.

Ben handed him the small blue booklet. The routine check went smoothly and several minutes later, they were parking in front of an office building. Entertainment apps on his smartphone were used to occupy James' ten-minute absence. The guards waved on their way out and the journey into the woods began. The first stop was to an outdoor adventure supply store for hiking boots, cargos, flannels, long socks and other wilderness necessities. Once that was checked off the list, Ben had the privilege to hold the auxiliary cord to play music for the remaining car ride. They began to bond over common tunes and new melodies shared between them. Funny stories from childhood, adult advice, and real talk mingled in the air around them. This energy was carried over into the small hike to a "mystical" lake that James kept raving about. Twenty minutes in, Ben was winded.

"Unc, how much longer is this little hike going to be? I think I'm starting to see colors," Ben exaggerated, leaning his weight onto the walking stick for balance.

"Oh, hush up. We're here now, crybaby," James teased as he held some branches back for them to walk through. On the other side was water clear glass as blue as the sky. Dusty copper boulders laced the background with golden shrubbery decorating it. The fragrance in the air was so authentic compared to the commercial air fresheners' imitation version. "Now you see why it was worth the wait?" He boasted proudly. This had been his hideaway for years now and sharing it with his nephew meant a lot to him.

"Wow, Unc, this is beautiful. It's so peaceful up here. How'd you find this place?"

"Chance really," he shrugged, leading them to a clearing. It was his usual set up area. They came prepared with foldable chairs, a blanket, food, and fishing poles.

The sounds of nature made the outing so peaceful. "So, is it true that music scares away the fish?" Ben asked. He had seen a few fishing videos on the web and couldn't hide his curiosity.

"Well yeah, to some extent. I heard if you play classical music, they respond to that."

"What about those brainwave songs? They help me relax sometimes."

"Binaural beats and yes, that would probably work too. I just like the silence when I'm out here, though. You get a much more intense experience that way," he answered, standing to stretch. "What do you know about increasing your brainwaves, little one?"

"Little? I'm nearly a grown man now, Unc. Just look at

me," he laughed. "And I know because I wander around into rabbit holes online a lot with an awesome laptop someone gave me."

James gave him a quick side-eye. "I hope you're wandering into the right ones. Remember I told you to use it for good."

Ben was quiet for a while as he thought about all the side hacking he and his friends had been doing back home. "Unc," he paused, questioning if he should come clean. James gave him his undivided attention. "What if I told you I did some little hacking…"

"I'd tell you to stop and to not get caught up in all of that mess. It's drama for someone at your age. I'm excited you're interested in technology, but give it some time. You'll be off to college soon somewhere doing amazing things. Maybe even get you a few government contracts and be set for life. Then you can help some little kid out too," he grinned at him. Ben nodded in agreement. "Can I ask why'd you do it?"

Ben sat silently as he mulled over the question. "Honestly, it gave me something to do with my friends and make some quick cash. I started after mom and dad split. I had extra time on my hands with no funds. So, we figured out a way."

"The kids I saw at your house? Y'all are a group of rough and tough street hackers?" he teased. "I mean, I get it. Trust me I do. But if we're being honest, you only did it because your feelings were hurt that your parents let you down. You have every right to feel some type of way. However, know you can't stay there forever. There's a big, blue world out there just waiting to be explored. Go travel and see what it's like. Work towards that, not doing stuff on the dark web. What's done in the dark always comes to light and usually, it's never pretty."

James' words sat heavy on Ben's chest as he reflected on his previous mindsets and behaviors. The silence of the wilderness allowed him to hear his inner thoughts and feelings perfectly clear. He knew what he was doing wasn't completely right, but it felt good. It was good enough to not focus on everything that was crumbling around him. *Maybe I should stop completely.* He had been on an unofficial break with C. Murphy and ignoring his messages.

"What do you know about counseling?" Ben asked in a low tone.

James sat his fishing pole down to look at Ben. "I know it's really helpful to have a professional available to walk through your emotions and thought process sometimes. We don't know everything and the counselors don't either. But they know enough to get you on the right track because, in the end, it's you that's going to have to do all the shadow work."

Confusion etched on Ben's face. "Shadow work?"

"You'll learn about it soon enough. Now c'mon, let's start heading home. It's going to get dark early soon." They packed up their belongings and left. Ben fell asleep in the car, thinking about everything his uncle said to him. He wanted to be a new *young* man.

A week had passed, and Ben had been busy picking up random books from around the house when he'd completed his school work. James had a collection of all genres, therefore giving him many options to choose from. Some days, he sat in the sunroom reading mystery novels. Others were self-help books in the office. Today, James found him in the game room, lounging on the sofa.

"So your mom called and said she wanted to come visit. You know, to make sure you're settling in good" James state, plopping down next to him.

Ben rested the book on his chest. " It'd be cool if my mom *and* the crew could come here."

"Just for the weekend. Fenty and Neyo's families won't say anything?"

"No. Fenty's mom is a nurse, so she usually works on the weekends. It's normally just them."

James thought about it for a moment. "Well, cool. Find me a date and I'll set everything up. I know your mom misses you."

"Yeah I kinda miss her too," Ben grinned, knowing she'd pinch him for that answer.

James just rolled his eyes at his nephew's humor. "Well look, I have an idea. How about we make a video game? Probably something in Virtual Reality. But when I say we, I really mean you."

"Unc-"

"Yeah, I know classes and whatnot, but you're chilling. Might as well make it profitable. I think you can do it."

"So what kind did you have in mind?"

"Mmm, something creative and out of this dimension. Like some otherworldly type stuff. Take people somewhere they've never been to before."

Ben smiled at his vision. "I think I see what you're getting at. I'll do some tinkering around." He stared off into space, thinking about the different sites he could visit to find some prepackaged code that he could modify. James exited the room, leaving designs swirling in his mind. The search engine's results were a long list of questionable relevance to the queue.

Makonnen: `Did you work for a C.`
`Murphy?`

Chills raced up his spine, freezing him instantly. Alarms began ringing in his head. A random account in an old chat room directly messaged him.

BigBeeKnee: `Who is this?`

Makonnen: `I don't mean any`
`disrespect. I just want to warn`
`you.`

The confusion was etched on his face. The hairs all over his body started tingling. He stared at the message for a second before the site indicated that the other person was typing.

Makonnen: `Look, I just want to find`
`my friends. We used to work for C.`
`Murphy and then we started getting`
`weird dreams. Then things started`
`happening. Now the two aren't`
`responding to any of our messages.`
`Just be careful.`

BigBeeKnee: `How did you find me?`

Makonnen: `The last accident was a`
`plane crash. System software`
`malfunction. But my team had just`
`written some simulated override`
`code for different aircrafts for C.`
`Murphy a few weeks before. I hacked`
`into the FBI to see their final`
`verdict. Security breach. Their`
`investigation had just an IP`
`Address from a house in Georgia.`

Your information popped up.

Ben's heart dropped. *I'm wanted by the FBI?*

BigBeeKnee: I have no clue what's going on, but how do I know any of this is real? So, you're saying C. Murphy is trying to set me up?

Makonnen: Whatever he's doing, you're involved. And if I know this, then others do too. Go off the grid for a while.

He started panicking. Usually, he'd be able to keep his cool, but this was completely out of nowhere. *I'm just a kid. What is going on?*

BigBeeKnee: Do you think they're going to come after me?

Makonnen: They'll probably think you're a regular 14 y.o. But I know if you're working with C. Murphy, then you're not an average kid. Just lay low.

Ben slumped in his seat once the chat availability bubble went grey. He didn't know that person, but appreciated them. His thoughts were focusing on tunneling himself out of this situation. Ben wanted to be mad at whoever this C. Murphy was, but knew there was no one to blame. He volunteered for the chaos. There was no thorough background check done on who he was working with; he just wanted the money. He just wanted the slim chance of finding some form of enjoyment. But now it was coming back to bite him. His chest ached as he just wanted to curl up and be a "child" again. He had been introduced to the real world with all its actions and reactions. Emotions flared as he wanted to do something. Anything. There was no way he could just take this laying down. He had been framed. C. Murphy underestimating him would eventually work in his favor. *I'm going to make him rue the day.*

After some moments of silence, strategies for action was devised. He messaged Fenty and Neyo to do a deep clean of their computers while he would do the same. They vowed to not work with C. Murphy again. The rest of the night, he crawled through the dark web for a VR simulator package. Just as he was ready to give up and have to build one from scratch, he stumbled onto a plain HTML page. The description sounded like what he needed. Taking a chance, he downloaded it. Hopefully, it would be the code that he needed.

Chapter 9: Ready or Not

A random weekend in September was chosen for the family visit. Luckily, they were able to pick similar arrival times so Ben and James picked everyone up from the airport at once. Ben hopped out to greet them and help put the luggage in the trunk. They traveled on the main road for some time until turning into a dirt road. Traveling up the long driveway gave them the same confusion Ben once had. When they arrived at the home, their eyes widened. Gathering outside the vehicle, they turned towards Ben for confirmation. He just nodded in amusement. By the time James finished the tour of the property, their jaws were hanging.

"So, this is why you were so quiet after you left," Fenty whispered to him, playfully bumping his shoulder.

"Yeah, it was like living in a resort. Time just kind of escapes you out here."

"I see," she nodded in agreement. They stopped in front of the large windows in the den. The woods provided an excellent covering from any unwanted guests. Tucked away in the solitude, they enjoyed pizza and chicken wings while watching a spy movie that Neyo recommended. It started getting late and the adults excused themselves to their rooms. The teens stayed in the den, lounging around a little while longer before they fell asleep there. Hours later, they awoke to the aroma of breakfast sizzling in a skillet. Old school jams were playing on the speakers throughout the house. The only plans they had for today were to sightsee around town and relax so they took their time getting ready for the day. The boys played video games while Fenty enjoyed the sauna downstairs and Kimberly worked on her laptop in another room. It was well into the afternoon when the crew came together for their excursion to downtown. Quaint mom-and-pop stores lined the town's square, ranging from small thrift shops to dry cleaners.

"So, this is it?" Neyo blurted out as they got back in the car, causing the others to laugh.

"Well, yeah. This isn't like the big city back home that y'all are accustomed to. It's more about nature here. Ben, tell 'em," James said, glancing at him in his rearview mirror.

Ben just playfully rolled his eyes while shaking his head. "Yeah, but it's not that bad. You have time to think."

"Who wants to do that," Neyo scuffed, looking out the window.

"Of course, he wouldn't," Fenty whispered to Ben.

"It's still some daylight out. We can go to one of the parks," James offered, getting ready to change routes.

"Or...we can get some lunch or something," Fenty suggested, feeling her stomach growl.

Everyone in the car agreed and James took them to his favorite Mexican restaurant. Chips, salsa, and laughs were passed around the large table. Ben looked up at his family and smiled, appreciating that he was able to have that moment with them. It had been a long time since he had felt that tingle of total bliss. It didn't feel fleeting, but he still closed his eyes, hoping it wouldn't all slip away. *Deep breaths.* His mom was cracking jokes like the old days while James hyped her on and the teens just watched. The staff was even joining in their fun by making jokes too. Good vibes were in the atmosphere. After a couple of hours, they packed up their to-go boxes and returned to

James' home. The group headed towards the den to relax with the crew trailing behind.

"So, do you know if your uncle is looking to adopt a child because I'm available. You know he could put a nice salon in here. I'd make it reeeaal-", Fenty rambled on before being abruptly interrupted.

"I need y'all advice on something," Ben butted in, guiding them by the elbows away from the adults and into the gym down the hall. He closed the door softly behind them and turned on the spotlights. Various workout machines and equipment filled the spaces. It looked professional. "I need to get a burner phone." He exhaled, finally getting it off his chest. Since the night he was messaged, he'd been thinking of how to get off the grid. Whoever C. Murphy was, was clearly very deep into the technological world, which was dangerous. *He's not going to catch me slipping anymore.* Ben knew he was up against an unknown challenge, but he had faith that everything would work out in the end. However, he was still nervous. Luckily, with his masterminds there in person, devising a plan would be a lot easier.

"I saw a gas station near the main road," Fenty spoke up first.

"Yeah, it looks hike-able. Maybe like thirty minutes," Neyo added, looking out the window. "The sun getting ready to set. We might need to borrow some of those flashlights I saw in the garage."

"I need to borrow some sweats and long socks. I refuse to be bit walking in these random woods," Fenty said, thinking about all the creepy crawlies. She had watched enough nature documentaries to know anything was possible and she didn't want to take any risks.

"Cool. My mom and uncle can't find out so we can meet by the back patio near the kitchen. We can walk around to the front and follow the road."

They all agreed. Neyo went to retrieve the flashlights and to change while Fenty followed Ben. Minutes later they were outside jogging down the driveway into the evening. They had to get there and get back as soon as possible. They had about an hour and a half before his mom would come, wondering where they were. Neyo was leading with Fenty in the middle and Ben keeping watch in the back. Even though it felt like a "serious mission", they were still whispering jokes and jabs at each other.

"Hey Ben, does this have something to do with that whole C. Murphy's situation?" Fenty asked, glancing over her shoulder at him. They had to keep their eyes on the ground to watch their footing. Large rocks, branches and holes covered with leaves were all booby traps. They couldn't return limping and avoid questioning.

"Maybe," he answered lowly. He felt bad because if anything happened, they told him beforehand that things could get crazy. The last thing he wanted to hear was "I told you so."

"So, should we be getting burner phones too?" Neyo questioned, stopping in his tracks.

Fenty ran into his back. "Boy, keep walking! Ain't nobody worried about us. He clearly had it out for Ben."

"Why do you say that?" Ben put his hand on her shoulder.

"Well, because we had been on the site for years, I never got a message. You just sign up and all of a sudden, you get a message. This was a strategic attack if anything."

Ben was silent in thought. He had never thought about it

like that. "But why me?"

"Only you would know that. I mean, what do I know? I could be wrong. I'm just saying, it all seems pretty ironic timing to me. "

A few moments of silence passed as they arrived at the convenience store. The outdated outside appearance made them skeptical. Walking in, they scanned the shelves looking for hanging, clear plastic containers. In the back were packs of individual flip phones with activation cards. They grabbed one, paid cash and ran out. The hike back to the house seemed longer than before as Ben mulled over Fenty's observation. *Was I really targeted?* Everything did seem so random and out of nowhere. He tucked the thoughts in the back of his mind for later. The sun had set by the time they arrived back at the house. They entered the same way they had exited and parted to their designated rooms.

Ben got in, hid the phone under his bed, showered and then laid down. He was tinkering around on his laptop trying to minimize some of the errors he was getting from his VR project when he heard light knocks on his door.

"You busy?" his mom said, peeking into his room. He turned around, shaking his head and waved her in. "Could we talk for a second? Feel like a weekend isn't enough time." She sat on his bed while he sat in front of her in a rolling chair from his desk. Kimberly wanted to freeze time. He was growing up so fast before her eyes. She could see his facial features and stature maturing. Her baby boy was becoming a young man. "So, from the emails I receive about your progress, you're doing amazing like I knew you would. Doing your work has never been a problem for you. Ever since you were a baby, I knew you were special. You started walking early. You were just smart. But don't get me rambling. How are you doing? What's been going on with you?"

"Mmm, nothing much. Just a normal kid with a normal life," he chuckled.

His mom gave him a suspicious look. "That's usually what an unusual kid living an unusual life would say, don't you think? Is there something you not telling me? I'm your mom, I know when something is up, Ben," she reminded, side-eyeing him. He gave her one of his famous grins. She rolled her eyes at how he always charmed her with that as a child.

"It's a virtual reality project. I'm trying to spawn different environments based on this equation. There are pre-packaged settings and stuff on the backend. I just can't get them to link for some reason." He spun around to look at his monitor and then back at his mom.

"That's really cool, Ben. I have no clue how you're doing it, but I trust you will figure it out. You always do." She looked around his room. "So, I need to tell you something now that you're older. Please don't be upset with me because I felt that it was in your complete best interest to not know. I didn't-"

"Mom, what are you talking about?"

"Benjamin, you have Asperger syndrome." She paused a few moments to let him digest her words. He focused on her with questioning eyes. "Supposedly, you have difficulties in social interaction and nonverbal communication, which I can see sometimes. But I never thought you needed to know because I didn't want you thinking it was a crutch. You are an outstanding, young man and besides a few bumps in the road, I couldn't have asked for a better son."

He cupped his right fist in his lap as he remained silent, analyzing the situation. "When did you first learn this?"

"We had you tested when you were younger. You probably wouldn't remember because it was nothing out of the ordinary; just some questions with your counselor."

"So, dad knew?"

"Of course. He didn't think anything was wrong, which it wasn't. As your mother, I could just tell you were different. You handled things differently than the other kids."

"So why now? Why tell me after all this?"

"I don't know the answers, I guess. I'm sure you're feeling things on the inside that you're not completely sure about, so this may be the bread crumb to your answers. I'm sorry that I hid this from you. I just wanted you to see that when you got older, labels don't mean anything. Society said that it'd be hard for you to have friends and communicate, but here you are. I'm sorry, baby, if you're mad at me. Hurting you was never my intention." Tears softly ran down her cheeks as she scooped him in for an embrace. Ben was kind of emotionless because he didn't really know how to respond so he hugged her back for comfort. "I love you. I wish I could stay longer." She put her head down in thought. "Well, I'm sorry again." She stood up, kissing the top of his head. She knew he wouldn't want to talk about it any further. Ben just sat there, pondering over the conversation. To get rid of the cloudiness in his chest, he went to spend the rest of the night with his friends. They stayed up talking and playing video games while watching movies.

The next morning was quiet as everyone prepared for the

departure. James suggested they go out for breakfast since their flights were later in the afternoon. He knew all the good food spots and wanted to leave a good impression. After eating, they headed towards the airport so they could avoid any last-minute distractions. Saying goodbyes were hard, but Ben knew they'd be back for the holidays. He watched them stroll through the glass doors and off into the hecticness. James started the car and drove them back to his home. Noticing Ben's demeanor, they went on a short walk through the woods in the back. Once Ben was back inside of his room, he locked the door and pulled the phone from its hiding place. Removing the activation card, he began setting up the phone. He sent a text to the phone from a website to make sure it was working. He didn't want it to have any trace back to him. Feeling satisfied, he slid the phone back under his bed and began working on his VR project.

A red bird fluttered quickly by the Browns Nuclear Plant in Alabama, which caused Dean Miller to stare aimlessly out the window. The early morning dispensed orange and golden stripes across the large lake next to the building. He yawned, tired of the break of day shifts that he had agreed to. Yes, it paid the bills, but he'd rather be out on the golf course with his college buddies or sleeping in. A small beeping noise brought him back to reality. Snapping his neck to the reactor's computer system, he moved the mouse to examine the issues. The beeping stopped and everything seemed normal. He leaned back in his seat and closed his eyes. Again, a small beeping alerted him of something in the system. This time, the screen was filled with red warning signs. His mouth dropped as he read the messages.

Just as he jumped up, his supervisor, Leon, ran into the control room.

"Dean, what is going on? The reactor!" he yelled, running to the computer. He tried adjusting the temperatures, but there was an executive override on the system. The reactor's core was overheating due to water draining back into the reservoirs. Dean looked on with wide eyes in shock. Speakers throughout the building called for the emergency team to report to the core chamber.

"I need to access the backup water tanks," Dean said to himself as he rushed to another computer. Leon was busy trying to shut down the override. Booting up the access program, he entered his credentials, only to have them denied. "Leon, quickly, come put your information in. It's locking me out!" Leon shuffled his feet in the rolling chair to enter his data. He too was denied.

"I.T. to control room immediately!" Leon yelled into the walkie-talkie. He scratched his head as panic set in. They didn't have long if the team couldn't manually cool down the reactor. They felt like sitting ducks. There had been plenty of "mistakes", but it had always been resolved quickly. However, this time, the clock was running out. They kept glancing at the time, awaiting a response from the technology specialists. Where were the people whose job it was to prevent this?

Something about this didn't sit right with Dean. "I'm leaving," he said as he hastily grabbed his belongings.

"Where are you going? We have to fix this!"

"There is no fixing this. This place is a ticking time bomb. We've clearly been hacked. We don't have access and we haven't heard back from the first responders." He glanced outside to see herds of people filing out the building. "Let's go. Don't lose your life for this job. We can still make it out."

Leon looked between Dean and the computer. "There's still time to fix this."

"Whatever man," Dean said, running out of the room. As he exited the building, a loud explosion erupted from the distance, releasing a dark cloud. The room that overlooked the reactor was up in flames. Dean clenched his hair as his knees buckled from the guilt. *He should've just come with me.*

"Aaarrghhh," Ben exhaled, frustrated by all the errors he was getting from the VR code compile. The equation he was using had little to no documentation but theoretically, it worked. Ben closed his laptop and closed his eyes. His head rested on his forearms as he meditated on how to solve this problem. Leaning up to stretch his hands above his head, a light bulb went off. He snatched his device back open and moved his fingertips rapidly across the keyboard. Slamming on the "enter" key, he waited for a few microseconds before seeing a clear dialogue box. No errors? He was pleasantly surprised but hesitant that it wouldn't run correctly. Shrugging it off, he put on the headset ready to see if the environment loaded. Looking through, he was standing in the middle of a grey room with infinite space and a black floor beneath him. Above his head were three white loading dots. Within seconds, the floor removed and he fell into a file room. The entire room was grey washed. Boxes upon boxes sat on shelves in rows that touched the ceiling.

So where in the world am I? He didn't remember adding this scene. Using the controller, he navigated going up the rows. A red box on the third shelf caught his eye. His name was written on it in big black letters. Looking around the room, he reached for the box. Inside were documents with his name on them and pictures from his web camera. The box was a case on him. There was a picture of him in his uncle's truck when they stopped at the base. Conversation records he had online with C. Murphy. *It's him.* Ben's breathing became more rapid and the room began to feel tighter. The rows of boxes pushed their corners into his chest until it was hard for him to breathe. Suddenly, he was dropped into the middle of a road. Black figures without faces marched in the same direction towards a large, glowing crater. It was the only color there. He felt like a moth to a flame as his legs reluctantly followed the crowd. As he leaned over to inspect the mystery, a big hand grabbed his face and pulled him in. Screaming, he pulled the headset off. His bottom hit the floor hard as he looked around his bedroom. Scrambling backward from the headset, he shook his head. His back touched the wall and a sense of relief washed over him Whatever the algorithm was spawning, he didn't create. *This is bigger than me.*

Chapter 10: Paris

Somewhere beneath the empty dark streets of Washington D. C., in the many underground facilities used by the government, the head of government for the United States of America sat at a table joined by other men and women. An extremely early morning meeting had been called. They had been hacked. Everyone had already been on high alert from all of the unknown random acts of violence committed against the citizens. Planes were crashing, facilities crumbling and the attacks appeared to be an inside job. Creating the level of destruction that had taken place would require specialized knowledge. Top investigators from multiple sectors of the government-- Federal Bureau of Investigation (FBI), National Security Adviser, Department of Homeland Security (DHS) Secretary, Head of National Security Agency (NSA)--sat with the President in deep contemplation. Hushed whispers amongst themselves, rustling from loose printer copies and tapping of keys occupied the space. The air was tense as wonder moved around them. They had not faced a series of attacks this suspicious in their lifetime. Technology was changing and developing uncharted territory that most were unaware of. A *ping* on the SmartBoard notified them of a message from an anonymous sender. President Evers used the mouse close to him to navigate the system.

"The imbecile is mocking us," he thought out loud. Before him, were coordinates and a *catch me if you can*. Clearly, the attacker had a death wish. He slowly rubbed his thumb across his index and middle finger, his nod of concentration beating to the rush between his ears. "He's teasing us."

"Sir, you think this could be a trap? According to the satellite, that's a property in Montana. Why would they send us there?" one of the investigators voicing the questions they all thought.

He paused for a moment. "Then we'll just go find out," he responded with a cold glare. "I want agents down there expeditiously." He returned to rubbing his fingers. Eyes watched in anticipation of his next move. "Whoever is there, I want them dead or alive."

Light taps on Benjamin's bedroom door stirred him from his comfortable spot in the bed. With his back facing the door, he turned his neck over his shoulder to greet his uncle. "Good morning, sorry about disturbing you. An old college buddy of mine in Paris is having a tech event next week. It's a fourteen-hour flight, but I'd love for you to come with me."

Ben sat straight up, eyes wide. "France, Unc?" he chuckled in disbelief. *He did not just casually offer me an out of the country trip.*

James smiled at Ben's excitement in amusement. "Yeah, every cultured young man needs at least two stamps in his passport book. But I'm assuming your answer is yes because I already bought your ticket?"

"Uh, yeah!" he jumped out the bed. His body was responding to the rush of joy. "When do we leave? What's the weather like? How much should I pack?"

"We leave later on this evening. The event is on Monday. I was thinking we could stay a few days afterward and tour the city. You should take a checked bag and dress for chilly rain. However, I got called into the base today for an emergency meeting, so we'll head to the airport when I come back. Be ready," he said, pointing his finger at him.

They pounded their fists and he walked out of the room. Ben sat on the edge of his bed, thinking about all the outfits he wanted to pack. Vacations that required planes made the trip even more special. Grabbing his large rolling duffle bag, he began throwing clothes, toiletries and shoes in. Seeds of possibilities sprouted in his mind about the endless opportunities for this trip to be a magical experience. He stopped arranging the contents of his luggage, gazing out the window. In a few hours, he'd be flying out of the country. Sun-bleached stone buildings, all symmetrical in shape, aligning historic roads. City lights glittering at night as they watch from above in the Eiffel Tower. Train rides to Versailles to see the Palace. Wandering the streets of Paris with a fresh, warm baguette tucked away for late nights at the hotel. Touches of modernness with hints of a classic feel throughout the hotel. He was beyond ready.

His energy was still raging as he looked around his room for something to occupy his mind. The VR headset caught his eye. Pausing a moment, flashbacks of grey blotches sent chills down his spine. He had been hesitant these last few weeks to work on it. Everything felt too real. Not virtual at all. *How* had all that information been collected on him? Something about it all unsettled his stomach. What was once butterflies was now motion sickness. He snatched the headset from his desk and placed it in the closet. Sitting down at his desk, he began backing up all his files on his external hard drive. All of the screenshots, documents and emails/messages between him and C. Murphy was uploaded to some old cloud space he still had access to. A small, still hum vibrated from somewhere deep within him as he stared at the screen before zipping and saving everything. Gathering all his evidence caused a deep sigh of relief to break the air as he pushed himself away from his desk. Scanning his room, he tried to remember if he forgot anything. He found his passport and threw it in his bookbag. Uncle James' return was unknown, so he decided on binge-watching some shows until it was time to go. Plopping on the sofa in the den, he turned on the TV. He drifted off an hour or so later, texting the crew about his Unc's big surprise.

Shaky limbs and a racing heart greeted him from his slumber as he scanned the room until it became familiar to him. Inflating his chest to capacity, he exhaled forcibly through his nostrils. He examined a bright sun with a drowsy haze as he dragged his feet back to his room. Entering it, he glanced at the closet. Muscles on his face twitched as he stared in contemplation. Something about the device was drawing him back. He still had questions. Tossing his phone on his bed, he retrieved the headset and began the program.

Ben's knees crumbled as he plummeted into a dirt patch. He released a sharp gasp once he focused on his surroundings. His eyes felt numb and there was no bright color--black, white and grey only. It was the fishing spot his uncle had taken him. *Okay, now I know something is up.* There was no grass, just rich brown dirt with dry areas. The dry areas cracked into large webs. The lake held no water, just fish skeletons still in tack. The mountains were grey with heavy pixilation. He reached his hands in front of him to touch them and they went through--palms feeling as if they were resting on jello. The trees were huge, having no ending or leaves. Long, dry branches circled their bodies and continued into the sky, which was a darker shade of grey but lighter than black.

"Enjoying yourself, Benjamin?" a familiar voice said over his shoulder. Turning his head in that direction, he met with a dark figure. The body was constructed as a human cloud of black smoke? He couldn't tell. "What? Not happy to see me?" sound just emitting from the object.

"C. Murphy," Ben called out in a flat tone.

"Darkness is fine now. I think we're on that friendship level, don't you say."

Friends? Ben twisted his face in disgust. "Look, what's going on? How are you in my *video* game?" He spat, his voice not hiding his irritation.

"Darkness is within you, Benjamin," he answered with questioning eyes. "Do you not know that Darkness is everywhere and *yoouu* helped."

Ben was not amused by its antics. "What are you?"

"I am Darkness. Anything else?"

"Why did you have all those files on me?"

"I didn't have them, *you* did. Don't you get it?" Walking closer, it reached, grazing the back of Ben's head. Ben lifted his actual hand to a warm sensation at the location. "You welcomed me in your life when you *wanted* to work with me. You manifested me. You wanted excitement away from everything and here I am."

"You caused the plane crash, didn't you?"

"We caused that plane crash."

"We?"

"Oui."

"Cut the cute stuff!" Ben screamed, losing his cool. Now

he was panicking He felt like he was out of breath. "What are you even talking about?"

"Of course, you wouldn't know what I'm talking about because you left your envelope," a gold shipping envelope floated in front of him. "This was a contract that you were negligent of even noticing. You just wanted what you wanted. But see, this here is our contract. You gave me the right to use you however I wanted to. So be ready, cause I had some fun."

"Have your fun because I'll have mine too. I have proof I did none of those things."

"Nobody will believe you," it hissed.

"Let's find out," he responded, removing the headset. Shutting down the system, he questioned the reality of the experience. *Darkness in my mind?* His chest felt uneasy and he sat on his bed in silence. The vibration of his phone pulled his attention back to the present.

"Uh hey Unc, what's going on?" he answered, rubbing his right hand over his face.

"Do you remember that meeting I was telling you about earlier?" James glanced over his shoulder at the group of agents that were standing behind him at the entry of their meeting room.

"Uh yeah?"

"Well, it was about how my property's coordinates and IP addresses keep popping up in their system. Would you happen to know anything about that?"

Ben's heart dropped into his stomach. He could've released his bowels right there on his bed. Instantly, he felt nauseous and oxygen depleted. His ears started ringing and he could hear James calling his name. "Unc, I can explain."

"Explain?" he almost shouted. Glancing over his

shoulder again, he pinched the bridge of his nose and exhaled. "Let me figure out some stuff. I might be longer than expected."

"Are we still going to Paris?"

"Yeah. Tony is sending over his jet. We'll go through the hangar entrance. Just be ready."

He hung up frustrated. Ben froze in panic. *It really did it.* He knew it was a reason why he had to collect all that information. Racing to his laptop, he threw it in his bookbag. In a haste, he threw on his hiking boots and started into the woods. Following the main road, he tried to remember how his uncle drove to the base. Brittle leaves crunched under his feet. The sun was setting and now he needed the flashlight in his pocket. Frigid winds scratched his exposed cheeks and brought tears to his eyes. Too many words and emotions swarmed him. The hike felt more like a chase from his mistakes. *My uncle can't pay for my attribution to this mess.* Forty-five minutes passed, but it felt like an eternity as he finally reached the barbwire fence. Brushing a spot with his foot, he sat there crossing his legs. Pulling out his computer, he opened his terminal to log into their network manually. Wifite sniffed it out, used a command to tap in, ran a password text file for several minutes, retrieved packets and then uploaded his secret weapon. Within seconds, a zip file containing everything he had pertaining to the whatchamacallit was flooding their system. Any computer connected to their network would have access to all of the dates Darkness hacked into accounts, their names, locations, the information Darkness initially presented and all files that were obtained from Ben's end. Hopefully, the right person would see it. Just as quickly as he logged in, he logged out. Now he had to race back to the house.

A bunker room beneath a desert that bordered Idaho and Nevada held the computers to five MQ-1 Predators. No overhead lights flickered on as the system came alive. A loading screen replaced the blank one. Green characters line the monitors neatly and were entered without any fingers tapping on keys. No warmth filled a single seat as the system unlocked the underground garage for the drones. Nearby stones rattled from the vibration of the hidden door cracking through years of settled dirt. Shrubbery was unearthed as an unmanned aircraft took flight, the engines burning and blowing everything in its path. With no pilot and traveling at 400 nautical miles, the system trusted the given coordinates to reach its destination in one hour.

The skin on James' knuckles stretched tightly as it could as he gripped the steering wheel and slammed on his brakes in his driveway. Things were getting messy and he needed to get to the bottom of it. He had been in the private contracting business for over ten years and not once had his place of residence been discovered. Now randomly, his home was going to be the center of attention. He had been sitting in a meeting room for hours being interrogated about his business and clients. How had *his* address been given? Who would want to set *him* up? Was there *anybody else* at the residence that needed to be questioned as well? James' poker face was as solid as stone. His answers short and sweet. He gave no more information than what was requested of him. No point in digging holes when he didn't know the full story. Unsatisfied with his answers, they wanted to still do a full investigation at his house. He was ordered to hand over his work laptop and remain on base until the investigation was completed. Luckily, he had friends in high places and the agents let him leave before the raid on his home began. However, he had no intention of staying around--just grab bags and leave. He knew things could get ugly and wanted to get them as far away from the madness as he could.

"Benjamin!" he shouted, rushing in. He jogged to his room to grab his luggage as he still called out for his nephew. Getting no response caused his brows to draw in. Pulling out his phone, he began dialing his number.

Benjamin stood at the top of the hill that overlooked his uncle's property behind his house. From up there, he could spot his uncle's car. Felling the buzz in his pocket, he retrieved his phone seeing it was James. "Hey Unc, I just stepped out for a second. I'm coming down from behind the house now," he stated. As he continued standing there, he could see a line of black SUVs approaching the house.

"You need to get back here immediately. We have to go," James warned into the phone. He carried his suitcase to the front door. Alarms in his home started signaling a presence in his driveway.

Nervously, Ben stood watching. He urged himself to run down the slope, but his legs wouldn't move. James repeatedly called his name but loud whistling above him drowned it out. Throwing his head up to observe, he saw a large air-to-surface missile bolt towards the house. Now he could move. "James! Get out of the house! Now!" he screamed in vain into the phone and squeezing it into his palm as he rushed down the incline. Slipping on damp leaves resting under the dry ones, he fell forward. His tumbling was halted by a fallen tree lying horizontally. His chest, forehead, stomach, chin and all slammed hard into the trunk. An explosion sent deafening ringing to his ears. Burning debris scattered the forest floor. He looked over the bark bench to see the home destroyed. It was just a plot of burning land and ruble. Everything within close vicinity was disintegrated instantly. The Hellfire missile did its job. The drone reporting *mission complete* as it returned back to its resting place.

"Noooo," Ben hollered from the depths of his soul. He had just watched his best friend be washed away because of his wrongdoings. His head cradled by the pile of leaves. He laid there holding himself as he cried, rocking. Tears and intolerable bellows flowed freely like a newborn baby. "James!" he screamed repeatedly, trying to sit up but kept feeling the waves of grief knocking him down. *Get up, Benjamin!* But he couldn't move. He was numb. His chest felt empty. *Get up, Benjamin!* Whatever was speaking to him urged him to start moving quickly. In the distance, he could hear crunching and men's voices.

Fighting through the crippling pain, he threw his arm over the bark to pull himself up. With trembling limbs and tears still in his eyes, he found the strength to crawl back up the hill and slide down. *They could be tracking you.* Glancing at the phone that was still in his hand, he smashed it against a tree. Limping to the main road, he began walking towards town. Getting closer, he pulled out his burner phone to call a taxi to take him to the hangar. The ride was short and the navigation to the private hangars was easy. He was able to bypass security without giving any personal information besides Tony being his point of contact. He reached the designated shed to find a small white plane. Two men were leaned against it. Once they noticed him, all parties stopped waiting for an introduction.

"Are you Tony?"

"Depends on who's asking," an older male said, folding his arms.

"I'm James' nephew."

"So, where's James?"

Benjamin crumbled. It was his fault he wasn't there to enjoy the trip with him. His uncontrollable sobs made the men side-eye each other. "They killed him," he repeated, pulling his knees to his chest, his feeling go beyond his physical.

"Who?" Now Ben had their attention. James was their friend and army buddy. They had seen things together that men shouldn't have when deployed together overseas. "What's going on?"

"I don't know. I just came home and it was going up in smoke," he blubbered.

"Come on, kid. Let's go," he said, ushering him on to the jet. With just his bookbag and the clothes on his back, Ben hurried onto the plane. The plane began taxing down the runway, as he quickly dialed Fenty's number.

"Hello?"

"I'm going to Paris and I don't know when I'll be back," was all he could get out before being told to turn off his cellular service. Buckling up, he laid his head back and closed his eyes. He couldn't keep the images of the explosion from replaying in his mind. *I'm so sorry, Unc. It wasn't supposed to happen like this.* His tears cascaded down his cheeks like rain. He clenched his bookbag closely to his chest as they took off with darkness surrounding them--the lights in the city glittering below. *It wasn't supposed to happen like this.*

Made in the USA
Coppell, TX
15 January 2020

14509387R00074